Bride to the Fiend Prince

REBECCA F. KENNEY

This book is a work of fiction. Names, characters, places, and incidents are the product of the author's imagination or are used fictitiously. Any resemblance to actual events, locales, or persons, living or dead, is coincidental.

Copyright © 2021 by Rebecca F. Kenney

All rights reserved. In accordance with the U.S. Copyright Act of 1976, the scanning, uploading, and electronic sharing of any part of this book without the permission of the publisher is unlawful piracy and theft of the author's intellectual property. If you would like to use material from the book (other than for review purposes), prior written permission must be obtained by contacting the publisher. Thank you for your support of the author's rights.

First Edition: September 2021, Rebecca F. Kenney

PLAYLIST

"Hate Me," Eurielle

"Scars," Boy Epic

"Armor," Landon Austin

"Closer to You," SVRCINA

"Can They Hear Us," Dua Lipa

"Wonder," Shawn Mendes

"Lies in the Dark," Tove Lo

"Fearless," Taylor Swift

"Don't Stop Holding Me," UNSECRET, Key Crashers, Ivory Layne

"No Good," UNSECRET, Ruelle

"I'll Be Your Hero," Tommee Profitt, Stanaj

"Pick Me Up," Sam Feldt, Sam Fischer

"Reign," Tommee Profitt, Anna Graceman

"Ever Ever After," J2

1

Papa always promised he would let me marry for love. He said it over and over throughout my growing-up years. "Even if I can do nothing else for you, Amarylla, I will do this. I will allow you to choose your husband."

I don't know why I believed him. He had broken a million promises to me before—little ones, like not coming to the tea parties I set out for him, or skipping my bedtime kiss, or attending a meeting instead of my birthday celebration. He was the king, after all. A busy man who could not be expected to have time for one tiny daughter.

With all those broken promises lying fragmented in my heart, the final and most terrible betrayal should not have come as a surprise. But it did, because he had promised that one thing to me for so many years—that my marriage would be my choice. I had intended to test him on it. I'd tried very hard to fall in love with the muscled stable boy who groomed my horse, so I could find out if my father truly meant it when he said I could have my heart's choice. But the stable boy was so very dull.

When I tried to talk to him, he only stared, with a vacant sort of smile, and made one-word answers; so I'd given up on that test of my father's promise.

But I still believed in it.

My father ate dinner with me that fateful evening. Eating a meal with him was a rare and wonderful occurrence, and I was too delighted to question it. I sipped the fancy foreign tea he'd handed me, and smiled at him across our plates of roast pork, tomatoes, mushrooms, and greens. We talked of little things, of the new horses and the refurbishments to the east wing, until I was halfway through my cup of tea and feeling oddly sleepy and detached. Perhaps I was more tired than I'd thought. Perhaps I should go to bed early. I blinked at my father, and my hand seemed to move in slow motion as I set down the cup.

His voice seemed to come from a great distance. "Tonight, you will marry the Prince of Terelaus."

"The Prince—of Terelaus," I said distantly, with difficulty. "The one they call a devil? A fiend?" And I tried to laugh, because I thought he was joking. The laugh dribbled between my lips, and I pressed my hand to my eyes as the room swam before me.

"It has all been settled. Your things are being packed, and your maids are here to prepare you." He lifted his hand, signaling to someone behind me.

The meaning of his words sifted through the haze in my mind. I struggled to think clearly, to process what was happening. My gaze dropped to the half-empty cup of tea. "You—you drugged—me…"

"I had no choice." My father wore a pained expression. "We've been at war with two kingdoms for too long, with Terelaus in the north and Ista to the west. The Terelonian forces have grown too vast and terrible to resist alone. People are dying, Amarylla—our soldiers, and the citizens of our border villages. I tried to make a treaty with Ista, to gain them as our allies against Terelaus, but they said no. To save lives I had no choice but to give in to Terelaus, to surrender. They will allow me to continue ruling, under supervision, if I make a grand gesture of loyalty. This is the only way, Amarylla, don't you see? You will be saving thousands of lives by this sacrifice."

He sounded as if he might be on the verge of tears, though with my brain dulled by the drug, I could not be sure. Honestly, I could barely understand what he said. I only knew that firm hands were gripping my arms, pulling me to my feet, dragging my leaden body along the palace corridors to my room. My head lolled and my eyelids drooped as I was sponged and coiffed, dressed in a beaded gown of white satin. My tongue and lips felt thick and swollen, and though I tried to speak the words came out as unintelligible mumblings.

Someone pushed open the door to my room. "The Terelonian sorcerer is here to take her."

I was propped on my feet and hustled from my chambers to my father's throne room. My father stood rigid, dressed in a crisp uniform draped in medals and chains. Under the freckles I'd inherited from him, he looked a shade paler than usual.

With him stood several members of our Court, and four strangers—two Terelonian guards, the Terelonian ambassador, and a masked figure in flowing dark robes that pooled across the tiled floor. I blinked, trying to clear my head. The tea seemed to be wearing off.

"No." I shaped the word carefully, forced it out. My body lurched against the hands holding me, but the resistance was weak and ineffective.

"They have said that I can come visit you." My father's voice was a plea for forgiveness.

I turned, met his eyes, and pushed out another word, full of hate and betrayal. "Don't."

My father stepped forward and embraced me anyway, and as he did he whispered in my ear, "Try to uncover the source of their magic."

I glared at him as he pulled away, as he made a great show of wiping his streaming eyes.

Try to uncover the source of their magic. The words thrummed in my dizzy head as my guards handed me over to the Terelonian soldiers, and my trunks and satchels were piled around us. The masked sorcerer walked in a circle around our little group, green light zipping from his hands, forming a domelike web of shining emerald lines. Then the sorcerer stepped into the dome with us, and lifted both arms.

A screaming, rushing wind raced around me, through me, dismantling my bones and skin, and I wanted to shriek but I had no air. With a jerk that I felt in the pit of my being, I snapped back together, whole again, but my skin still crackled with the aftereffects of the traveling magic.

We had spun through the air, from place to place, transported in less than a minute. The web of green lines receded, melting into the glossy black lake of tiles on which I now stood.

And by accident or the sorcerer's malicious intent, none of my trunks or satchels had been brought along with us. I'd been exiled with nothing but the clothes I wore.

Black pillars arched upward, so tall I could barely make out the ceiling overhead. Those black pillars were studded with glowing amber crystals, the only light in the Cursed Palace of Terelaus.

This cavernous place was to be my new home. And in a few moments, I would be married to the Fiend Prince.

2

The drug my father had given me was wearing off. I only swayed a little as I walked through the vast dark halls of the Cursed Palace. I could probably run if I tried. But where would I go? Whole forests and mountain ranges lay between me and my home now. Terelonian sorcerers traveled by magic rarely, in times of great need or importance. It was unlikely I could find one willing to take me back home, even if I could give the slip to the grim-faced guards flanking me on either side, or the sorcerer stalking ahead of me.

We passed beneath an archway of braided bones and entered the throne room. Between long double rows of black columns, against a twisted mass of metal and stone and dark glimmering crystals, stood the Seat of Ghast, a throne cut and compiled from the skeleton of some monstrous ancient creature, unearthed in the wastelands of Terelaus. It looked every bit as forbidding as the two figures standing before it on the raised dais. One bore a heavy crown of onyx, with long gray hair flanking a smooth black mask. That must be the king of Terelaus, the Dreadlord himself. The other figure, slightly taller, wore a hood, and his mask bore a demonic leer. The Fiend Prince, no doubt.

A third figure approached, wearing no mask. I smiled, relieved to see another face, and a woman at that—but her dark features were sober, and she looked me over without sympathy. Her headdress, twice as tall as the king's crown, was studded with pale gems.

"Approach the Seat of Ghast," she intoned.

I lifted my eyebrows. With the drug haze dissipating, my tongue was as agile as ever. "Why do you people give everything such doleful titles? Seat of Ghast, Cursed Palace, Fiend Prince, Dreadlord." I released a faint chuckle. Humor was usually my backup plan when I was in trouble, my comfort space when I was nervous. But the people around me did not react—except that the black-gloved fingers of the Fiend Prince twitched slightly. As if he couldn't wait to get his filthy hands on me.

All my humor drained away. "I did not agree to this marriage," I said. "I do not consent."

A low raspy voice issued from beneath the king's mask. "Your father has given his consent. We do not need yours."

"He doesn't own me. He cannot do this. You have to let me go—I only found out about this at dinner—" The guards' hands closed around my upper arms and I jerked against them, snapping into fight mode instantly. My father had been wise to drug me. I had achieved top marks in every combat course I'd ever taken.

I used the guards' grip for balance as I swung outward with my leg, smashing my foot into the right-hand guard's kneecap. He groaned and bent, and when his grip loosened I popped my arm free, following up with a quick blow to his throat with the side of my hand. I whirled, swinging the left-hand guard around, slamming his body into a third guard behind us. While they were struggling to right themselves, I faced off with the fourth guard, faking a blow, dodging under his attempted block, and landing a solid kick to his groin.

All of that took more breath and effort than usual, thanks to the cursed satiny skirts weighing me down. I hoisted the gown and started to run, but a net of slim green whips curled around my limbs. As soon as they impacted my skin I was petrified, frozen in place. My body revolved slowly around as the sorcerer dragged me toward the dais, like a fish on a line.

My limbs wouldn't obey me, but my mouth was free. I let loose with the most depraved and disgusting of curses, every foul word I knew and some that I invented on the spot. Maybe if I behaved horribly they would deem me unfit to marry their prince and send me home.

No such luck. The sorcerer whipped another cord of magic across my mouth, and it nestled between my lips, burning and buzzing across my tongue. The lines of green light around my body tightened, painful and hot. I tried not to make a sound, but tears pooled in my eyes in spite of my resolve, and I glared through them, hating myself for the weakness.

The ceremony that followed was half in Common Tongue, half in some Terelonian ancestral dialect. Apparently I was promising reverence and obedience to my husband. I was agreeing never to withhold my body for purposes of pleasure or procreation, never to so much as look at another man, never to leave his side without his permission—all sorts of nonsense. I tried to form words again, to protest, but the burning cord of magic between my jaws thickened, scorching my tongue so sharply I yelped with pain.

"Andreas." The voice came from the Fiend Prince's mask. At the word, the sorcerer's line of magic thinned again, cooling slightly. It was a welcome mercy, but I doused any fleeting sensation of gratitude. The Fiend Prince was marrying me against my will. A truly kind and good fiancé would have demanded that I be unbound and allowed to speak.

When it came time for me to affirm the vows, the woman reciting them paused for half a second, and the sorcerer flexed his magic, bending my neck in the semblance of a nod. "Assent is given," droned the woman, and moved on to the Fiend Prince. He assented with a sharp jerk of his head. "Assent is given," she repeated, and moved into the final words, "You are now bound by mettle and magic, by ichor and ice, for pain and pleasure, soul to soul and blood to blood."

The king stepped forward, impatience in the hard angles of his shoulders. "Take her to his bedroom."

"Yes, Dreadlord." The sorcerer headed for a hallway, dragging me along by my magical green leash.

As we left the throne room, I heard the king say to his son, "You must ensure her compliance tonight. Call the physik if you need something to sedate her."

Panic raced along my nerves, and more tears trailed along my cheeks as I felt my own wretched helplessness. How I hated magic! So unfair. Without that advantage on their side, they could not have subdued me so easily.

Try to uncover the source of their magic. My father's secret words grated against my mind. Why hadn't he warned me what he was planning? What hadn't he given me more information, more time, more consideration—

The horrible truth of it was that he didn't care enough. That he was willing to give me up for the sake of his precious people—sell me to Terelaus and give me a last-minute, half-assed directive to spy on my new husband and his father.

Well, I wouldn't be doing any favors for my father. And I'd be damned if I allowed the Fiend Prince to dose me into "compliance" tonight.

3

The sorcerer pushed me between a pair of ornately carved ebony doors. Then he kicked me, full in the rear, and I sprawled on my face on the floor, unable to break my fall since my arms were still bound with his magical ropes.

"Brintzian scum," he snarled. "Wretched whore. You're not worthy of carrying the heir's seed. Know that if you attempt to bring harm to the Fiend Prince tonight, I'll slice off some precious little parts of you. You'll never be the same again."

The door slammed, and the magical lines around my body vanished.

A low fire glimmering in the grate yielded the room's only light, and its orange glow didn't reach far, because the Fiend Prince's bedroom was immense. It was so heavily swathed in shadow I could only guess at its dimensions. The hiss and pop of the flames comforted me, a familiar sound in a room heavy with dark drapery, opulent floral scents, and a carpet so plush that when I sat up, my hand sank into it.

It would not be long before the Fiend Prince came to me. Even if he was reluctant to do so, his father seemed like the type to hurry him to the consummation. Apparently Terelaus was desperate for an heir, though I couldn't think why. The king seemed healthy enough, and the prince was rumored to be a fearsome warrior. Difficult to tell what state they were in with the masks, though. Perhaps they were hiding some terrible encroaching disease. I shuddered, thinking of sharing a bed with the diseased body of the Fiend Prince, thinking of scabrous hands crawling over my body—

No. No, that could not happen.

I lurched to my feet and began hunting through the room, looking for anything I might be able to use as a weapon. The fireplace tools were an obvious choice, but also harder to conceal. Stealth would be my only friend in this endeavor.

At last, in a bottom drawer, I located a pretty little jeweled dagger, probably the brightest and most cheerful thing in the room. It lay half-concealed by some of the prince's underthings— soft black shorts and one pair of scarlet silken drawers. I pushed those aside and pulled out the dagger, delighted at its feel and craftsmanship. A little light and frail perhaps, clearly meant as a decorative piece—but its blade was sharp enough when I tried it against my thumb. It would do the job nicely.

The Fiend Prince's bed matched the scale of the room, a horrifying, haunted castle of a thing with towering twisted spindles, draped in curtains the color of ink and blood. A gauzy black negligee lay across the sheets. I couldn't very well climb into the bed in my ridiculous wedding gown, and I would die before I'd put on that bit of silken shadow. I divested myself of the dress and shoes and slid between the sheets in my corset and lace pantalettes.

I'd chosen the bed as the best place for the assault. When the Fiend Prince entered he would likely be on the alert, ready to fend off a full-on charge or a sneak attack from behind the door. Lying on the bed would give him the impression that I had given in, that I was ready to submit. He would approach me smugly, read to take his prize, and then—I'd give him a surprise instead.

Dragging the sheet over myself and renewing my grip on the dagger, I lay still, while my heart thrummed frantic.

When would he come?

When?

Damned prince. He should get his sorry ass in here, and quick.

What if he never came? What if I had to wait all night? What if I fell asleep and dropped the dagger and—

The door opened, slowly, and gradually. Yes, the Fiend Prince was on the alert. My attack on his guards in the throne room had shown him I was not someone to underestimate. I left my eyes open only the tiniest of slits, peering through my lashes. I hadn't drawn the bedcurtains, so I could make out his dim, distant figure by the door.

"It's all right," he said to someone, probably his guards. "She's in bed. Remain just outside, and listen in case I call you."

Someone voiced a muffled protest, but the prince repeated, "It's all right."

He closed the door and heaved a sigh. Fabric shifted as he took off his hooded cape and tossed it over a chair. Boots thumped to the carpet, one after the other. Then the Fiend Prince walked toward the bed, unlacing his shirt. I let my eyes seal shut. My fingers tensed around the dagger hilt, but I forced my body to relax, to look soft and pliable and non-threatening. I kept my face smooth, as if I were sleeping, and I breathed evenly.

For a long moment there was no sound or movement. Only silence, and the dark scent of the wine-colored flowers on the bedside table, and the gentle huff of my own feigned breathing.

The Fiend Prince was just standing there, looking at me. I had only drawn the sheet up partway, so he was likely enjoying the generous view of my breasts. The cups of my corset only hid about two-thirds of my assets, leaving plenty on display.

Take your last looks, I growled internally. *You're about to die.*

Warm fingers brushed my shoulder.

My hand launched at his throat, a vise grip, choking off the air he might use to cry out, and as I lunged upright I forced him down to the mattress. It was so smooth and sudden he had no chance to shout before the tip of my dagger pressed to his jugular vein.

He'd been surprisingly easy to overcome—lighter than I expected, less muscular. Was he not the mighty warrior everyone thought him to be?

I couldn't see his face. He still wore the leering mask. Still and quiet he lay beneath me, not a hint of fight in him, though his breath wheezed through his constricted throat.

"You'll not touch me again," I hissed. "Not ever, do you understand?"

4

The Fiend Prince struggled to speak through my chokehold, behind the grated mouthpiece of his mask. "I was only—going to wake you—so I could speak to you."

I eased my grip slightly, and only because he had rebuked the sorcerer who was burning my tongue. "Liar. Your father wants you to consummate. He told you to drug me if you had to."

"I intended no such thing, Princess." Now that he wasn't choking, his voice was young, light, and masculine in a way that quickened my blood. I was suddenly conscious that I had ended up astride him, leaning over him, with my breasts surging a little too far out of the confines of my corset.

"Take off your mask," I said.

"That, I cannot do."

"Why? Are you so disfigured that your face would make me scream? I'll wager I have more courage and compassion than you think."

"I don't doubt it. But I cannot remove the mask now. Tomorrow, perhaps."

I pressed the dagger more firmly to his flesh. "Now, else you die."

"You would kill me then? Spill my blood here in our bed, on our wedding night?" There was a wry, bitter twist to his words. "Did it ever cross your mind that this marriage was not my idea, or my wish? That perhaps I was also taken by surprise, and forced to go along with it?"

"You seemed willing enough, when you stood beside your father the Dreadlord and gave your consent," I spat.

"Words only," he answered. "They did not reflect my heart, or my desire."

"You're only saying this because you want to live."

He sighed heavily. "Believe what you like. And sit on me as long as you like. Now that my shock is fading, I'm becoming very accustomed to your presence." He shifted his hips slightly under me, and I felt the roll of hard flesh as he moved.

I had done saucy things with the dull stable boy, so I recognized the shape and feel of that hardness in the prince's trousers—though to be honest, the stable boy's piece had been rather on the small side, barely enough to close my hand around. This felt like *more*, in the best way, and I hated that I was curious what it might look like, feel like—

"Pervert," I said haughtily, as if my own body weren't heating at that very moment. I bent closer, shifting the dagger so the edge of its blade lay against his voicebox. He swallowed, his throat flexing beneath my fingers.

"Ah yes, lean in a little more—just like that," he said. "Such a wonderful view."

I glanced down, where my chest was spilling out of the corset. "Damn it. This one wasn't meant to contain so much as to—push everything up." I straightened, adjusting the corset with one hand, keeping the blade pointed toward him, its tip hovering over his heart this time. His shirt lay unlaced, gaping in a wide V, exposing a thin pale chest. A lean chest, but not a powerful one, not heavily muscled and sculpted like a warrior's body should be.

"I like your corset," said the prince contentedly. "But if you need other undergarments, or anything else, I'll see that you get it."

"In exchange for what?"

"Well—you've made it clear that I'm not supposed to touch you—though it seems you'll make free touching me wherever and whenever you please. So perhaps we could find some other arrangement. Let's see—my father wants to know that we've consummated our marriage. What if you help me convince him that we have?"

I stare down at his leering masked face. "Lie to the Dreadlord?"

"You were about to murder his only son. A small lie seems far more reasonable, don't you think?"

"I—"

"Come, wife, help a husband out."

Instantly I drove the dagger point through his skin—just the tip, just enough to release a few beads of blood. "Don't ever call me *wife* again."

"Ow," he said. "I might have to, in public."

"What makes you think I will ever agree to appear in public with you? I'm going to kill you and leave your body for your father to find. And then I'll escape, and go home."

"How? How will you find your way through the maze that is the Cursed Palace? How will you avoid the guards, and the sorcerers, and the magical wards? How will you traverse the wilderness, cross the mountains, and forge the rivers? Forgive me, Princess, but though you're a skilled fighter, you don't seem like the type to have trekked far on foot through strange lands."

I tried to swallow down the uncertainty that rose with his every question. "Then I will keep you as a hostage, and force someone to give me an escort home."

He shook his head. "The instant you cleared the palace grounds, they would only recapture you. My people have no honor, and would adhere to no bargain they made with you. Besides, our sorcerers could easily disengage me from your grasp."

"Could they stuff your blood back into your body once I spilled it?" I retorted.

He shrugged against the sheets. "Maybe. How much do you know of our magic?"

My father's words echoed in my brain again. *Try to uncover the source of their magic.*

"I know plenty," I said boldly.

The prince chuckled, the sound as fiendish as his mask. "You're very brash and savage and angry. Not what I expected at all."

"And what did you expect?"

"Not someone who could take out three of my father's guards."

"Four." I slid off him, sitting crosslegged on the bed. But I kept my knife hand on my knee, ready.

"Four," he agreed. "And you're far more beautiful than I could have hoped. Not that it matters," he added quickly, "because I won't be touching you. There will be nothing between us— except, I hope, a mutual arrangement. A pact, one royal to another."

"I'm listening," I said. "What do you want?"

5

With my dagger no longer at his throat, the Fiend Prince sat up. He dabbed a finger to the place on his chest where I'd pierced his skin. "You stabbed me."

"Only a little. Don't be a baby about it."

He chuckled again, and I almost smiled before I caught myself. *Fiend Prince*, I reminded myself sternly. *Bad man. Enemy.*

"What I want is quite simple," he said. "My father wants reassurance that we're trying to create an heir. So you need to help me convince him that we have been intimate."

"Why the desperation for an heir? Are you on your way to an early grave? You do look a little pale, and weak."

He splayed long fingers over his chest. "That hurts, Princess, it really does."

I shrugged. "I'm only saying what I see."

"Your brutal honesty gives me hope," he said dryly. "I cannot tell you why my father is so desperate to secure the future of our line. You see, I don't trust you yet. I know, I know—it's very strange. When women brandish daggers at me I usually spill all my darkest secrets, but with you—" he shook his head— "I just don't feel that trust that a husband should feel for his wife. Maybe if you climbed on top of me again—"

"I could cut you somewhere else, if you think that would help." I twitched the dagger in the direction of his crotch, and he swerved his hips away quickly.

"Emasculating me would be counter-productive, I assure you," he said.

"Fine. So you want me to pretend to be your dutiful wife who provides you with full access to her body every night, is that it?"

"Exactly."

"And in return, what do I get?"

"You get *not killed*." He cocked his head aside, and that leering mask of his suddenly looked dreadfully sinister. He could shout for his guards at any moment and tell them I tried to assassinate him. I'd be restrained, punished, maybe imprisoned, or tied to the bed so he could have his way with me. Worst case scenario, the Dreadlord would decide I was more trouble than I was worth, that he could find another womb for his son to fill, and they'd kill me. My father had already surrendered everything; he could do nothing to save or avenge me.

"That got serious, didn't it?" said the Fiend Prince, rising from the bed and shucking off his pants. I eyed his pale legs, scattered with dark hair. He pulled the shirt off as well, and my gaze snapped instantly to a knotted, coiled mess of scar tissue along his left side. The scars began just under his left pectoral and traveled all the way to his hipbone. When he turned, I saw that they wrapped around his back, nearly crossing his spine.

"I showed you mine," he said quietly. "Care to show me yours? Or perhaps you don't have any scars quite so hideous? It's not a competition, you know, Princess. Feel free to share."

"I have a few," I said. "From training. What's yours from?"

He went to the foot of the bed and pulled the curtains, blocking out most of the light from the dying fire. In the gloom, his mask looked more frightening than ever. "From a monster. Now, Princess, it's time to fulfill your side of the bargain."

"What—what do you mean?"

"We have to make my father think we coupled. And to do that, we have to make certain sounds, so the guards outside can bear witness."

"Sounds? Like me screaming for mercy while you plow into me?"

"Devil's bones, no! What is wrong with you?"

I shrugged. "Those seem like the most likely sounds for a woman forced into a marriage bed."

"No, you should make sounds of pleasure."

"Because you are so damn charming that I fell for you in less than an hour? Won't that seem a little—far-fetched?"

"Women have fallen for me in less time. Men too. I am a *prince*. That makes me innately desirable."

My jaw dropped. "Men too?"

"Would that displease you, if I'd been with men as well?"

"I—no, I suppose not—unless you prefer them solely, and that's why you want this arrangement."

"If I preferred men, I wouldn't have been ogling your breasts earlier. No, Princess, my tendency is toward women. And let's assume that you, being the vulnerable female you are, have succumbed to my beauty and charms—" he gestured to his lean, scarred body— "and you're caught in the throes of the best pleasure you've ever had." There was a bitter hardness to his tone when he referred to his own charms. That self-deprecation might have softened me a little, except I was too busy frantically trying to think what sounds I should make. I had never heard a woman "in the throes of pleasure," as he said, and I had never experienced such pleasure myself. When I'd been with the stable boy, he'd reached his climax quickly, long before I had a chance to get more than mildly excited, and the coarse grunts he made weren't something I wanted to imitate. I had tried to reach the pleasure peak myself, but I never seemed to find the right rhythm before I was interrupted or I fell asleep. So I was left staring blankly at the Fiend Prince, with my mouth slightly open.

"Do you not know what sounds to make?" he asked. "Are you a virgin?" He seemed shocked. "But—you're twenty-something, yes? You can't be a virgin—"

"No, I'm not a virgin," I said. "But I don't know how I would sound, because I've never—" I broke off, hating the rising flush in my cheeks.

"Did your lovers not try to please you?" His voice was softer, almost pitying.

"I am not discussing my lovers with you," I said haughtily. "Why don't you make the sounds at first, and I will do what you do."

"Very well." He climbed back onto the bed. "Follow my lead."

6

The Fiend Prince sat cross-legged among the pillows. His face was still concealed, so when he threw his head back my gaze lingered on the prominent tendons of his throat, the lump of his Adam's apple between them, and the clavicles below. Thin as he was, unimpressive though his build might be, there was something vulnerable and appealing about the angles of those sharp bones, and about the way his ribs showed faintly through his pale skin.

A loud moan broke from him, and I jumped, startled out of my admiring reverie. "Gods! Are you hurt?"

"Hush, idiot," he hissed at me, and he moaned again, louder, this time with a throaty male rasp that sent little tingles of arousal into places I had no business thinking about while sitting on an enemy's bed. "Oh, merciful maker, Princess, you feel so good!"

Blood roared into my cheeks. Of course this was part of the ruse we'd agreed upon. And now I was supposed to make noises, too. His noises sounded somewhat akin to pain—maybe if I pretended I was training, getting beaten down by my friend and fighting partner Ashari— "Oh," I moaned, "Oh, oh, ow—"

The Fiend Prince clapped a hand over my mouth. "Less *ow*, and more like this." He released a series of sharp, breathy cries, and my heart skittered through my stomach.

I gripped his wrist in my hand, conscious of how fragile his bones felt in the circle of my strong fingers. "I told you not to touch me." I tightened my grip slightly, and his fake moans of ecstasy took on a note of actual pain.

"There," he whispered. "You hear the difference? Come on, now—with me—" he kept gasping and moaning, and I imitated him as best I could. It was impossibly strange, sitting on the sheets with a masked stranger dressed only in his undershorts, mimicking the noises of lovemaking. Finally he gave a long groan of satisfaction, and I echoed it with a weak one of my own, and we were done.

"That was terribly unconvincing," said the Fiend Prince in a half-whisper, settling onto the pillows and drawing the sheets over himself.

"I know," I replied. "You sounded nothing like a man being pleasured."

"Oh no, Princess—*I* was a consummate actor. I deserve an award. You, on the other hand, sounded like a sick goat being skewered up the ass."

"I was imitating *you*!"

"But women are usually much shriller, you know, and sometimes they squeak, or mew, or scream—"

"Not likely," I managed.

"You sound a bit shaken, Princess."

"Only because I'm so embarrassed for *you*, making a fool of yourself like that." I lay down, keeping my dagger pointed in his direction. "You should be a gentleman and sleep on the sofa over there."

"Sleep on the sofa? In my own quarters? When I'm newly married?" he scoffed. "Not a chance. And you won't be taking the sofa either. If you want any measure of freedom in this palace, you'll pretend to be my pleasant and dutiful wife. And I'll take my birthday dagger back now."

"Birthday dagger?" I looked down at the small jeweled weapon I held.

"A gift from my mother before she passed. Hand it over."

Dread curdled in my stomach. "You're liable to pounce on me in the night if I give up this weapon. You told me yourself that your people have no honor and don't keep their bargains. How can I trust you to uphold our agreement and not touch me?"

"Oh, Princess, I have not the slightest interest in touching you. I may have been momentarily dazzled by the copious offerings of your corset, but I'm back in control of my senses now, and I must confess, you don't appeal to me at all. I generally prefer dainty, delicate ladies—not buxom women who are stronger than me."

Why did his words feel like the lash of a whip? "I thought you were a great warrior," I retorted, settling my head on the pillow, still gripping the dagger hilt. "But you're obviously not."

"Oh, I am—or I—I was."

His tone was layered with emotions I couldn't decipher through the mask. I was desperately curious about his face, and I wanted to see his eyes, too—I hadn't caught more than a glimmer deep in the dark eyeholes. I'd wait until he was asleep and then take his mask off.

Closing my eyes, I pretended to drift off, and I waited for his breathing to settle into a somnolent rhythm. It was hard not to give in to sleep myself—it had been a long day even before I'd been bundled into a wedding dress and magically transported to an enemy kingdom for an arranged marriage. But I could not fall asleep here, in the bed of the Fiend Prince of Terelaus, deep within the Cursed Palace. That would be terribly foolish. I must stay alert, vigilant, on guard.

Finally, finally, the prince seemed to have sunk into dreams, and I sat up, laying aside the dagger. I could make out the edges of the mask in the gloom. Gingerly I reached for it.

"If you remove it," said the Fiend Prince, "I will bed you in truth, whether I find you appealing or not."

Alarm flooded my nerves, and I retreated, nearly tumbling off the edge of the bed. The Fiend Prince chuckled. "Only a joke. Maybe. Go to sleep, wife."

"Don't call me your wife," I snarled. "You are not the husband I wanted. *I* prefer big gleaming warriors with abdominal muscles like the Oreyan Hills and skin with some *color*, not this dead fish-belly white of yours. You're barely more than a skeleton, just some fragile bones and a bit of pale skin."

He sucked in a quick breath, but he answered smoothly, "I'm well aware."

"And you won't tell me what's wrong with you?"

"I've only just met you. And I'm disliking you more by the second."

"The feeling is emphatically mutual," I snapped.

"Go to sleep."

"You first."

In the end I wasn't sure who fell asleep first—only that when I woke up, the Fiend Prince was peering down at me in the faint light of a sickly dawn, holding the jeweled dagger in his hand—and he wasn't wearing a mask.

7

The Fiend Prince had a shock of glossy black hair, swept back from a high, pale forehead. Thin dark eyebrows arched over deep-set eyes—I couldn't quite determine their color. He had a neat straight nose and cheekbones that looked as if they might cut through his skin any second. His crisp jawline swept down to a chin with a slight cleft. But it was his mouth that caught my attention—sweet gods, his mouth—beautifully full and pliant and kissable. I'd never seen such a pretty mouth on a man.

"Good morning, my sweet little wife," he said, with a sardonic hitch of those beautiful lips.

I scrambled upright, conscious of my scantily-dressed state and the snarled mess that had once been my wedding-night coiffure.

"You needn't get up," he said. "You won't be required until tonight's gala, at which the entire kingdom will celebrate our marriage properly. It may have been certified and consummated in secret, but now my father is eager to make it widely known. And he'll be equally eager for us to keep working on that all-important task of producing an heir."

"So I'm nothing but the bakery oven for the royal loaf," I muttered, swinging my legs out of the bed. As I stood up and straightened, every cell of my skin prickled with the awareness of how close I was to the Fiend Prince. It was my inner alarm, my personal threat gauge kicking in. Nothing more. Certainly nothing illicit or tingly, even though he still wore only the undershorts, and his thin body had a spare, severe beauty to it—

Amarylla, I scolded myself. *Shut up.*

"You think *you* feel objectified?" The prince snorted. "I'm only the yeast for the dough. It's my father's loaf, you see. He'll take whatever child we produce, and—" He cut himself off. "But no need to worry. I won't be injecting my seed into that hot little womb of yours anytime soon. Not *ever*, if I have any say in the matter. The servants will be in soon to bring us breakfast, and I wanted to be sure we are still in agreement about our ruse. You will pretend that you coupled with me, and in return I shall ensure that you have whatever you want—clothes, books, pretty dresses, jewels—"

My brain was still circling the phrase "hot little womb" and wondering if I was offended or aroused by it—but when he began listing the things I might want, I stiffened. "How about a training space and some equipment for exercising?" I asked.

He quirked an eyebrow. "You want to exercise?"

"I enjoy it. It calms me. When I don't burn enough energy I get a bit savage."

"More savage than last night?"

"Much more."

"Very well. I'll see what can be arranged."

The door behind him opened and he quickly leaned in to kiss my cheek—a show for whoever might be entering the room. He smelled of something dark and sharp and exotic, with a bitter twist—licorice, pepper, and myrrh. But his lips were petal-soft against my skin.

"A most satisfying night," he said, loud enough for the servants to hear. I managed to give him a fake simpering curtsy before he turned and walked toward a doorway, with a commanding, "Jai! Dex! My clothes!"

Two of the servants hurried with him into what I assumed was the bathing and dressing area of the suite. I followed timidly, because my bladder was aching. The Fiend Prince was standing in a long room lined with clothes, and as I crept past on my way to the washroom, he dropped his shorts and I got an eyeful of a very firm and nicely shaped backside.

The bathing area offered little in the way of privacy, since it was designed for the prince's sole use. I used it quickly, washed, and found some of my cosmetics and personal items set out on a little stand near the sink. I wasn't surprised that the Cursed Palace had running water—most royal families had access to emerging technologies. My father had always vowed to get running water into every Brintzian home—but with the war efforts draining our coffers and workforce, his vision hadn't taken shape. Another promise he had not been able to keep.

Maybe now, with the war over thanks to my marriage, our people could have improved plumbing systems. That is, if Terelaus didn't tax us unbearably—which they were likely to do. The Dreadlord didn't seem the type to hold sway over a nation and not ask for a share of its goods.

When I had washed up, a servant guided me to a back section of the prince's enormous closet, where a few gowns had been hung on a metal rack. I raised my eyebrows. "Where are the pants? The shirts?"

"Excuse me?" The servant looked confused.

"I'm used to having training clothes, comfortable clothes. Breeches, leggings, tunics, blouses?"

"All royal females wear lovely gowns in the Cursed Palace," said the servant meekly. "Are these not to your liking?"

"They're all right." I trailed my fingers over the material—dark, heavy velvets and brocades, all except for one white gown, an off-the-shoulder style with a sweetheart neckline and silvery swirls all over its surface.

"That one's for the celebration tonight, Your Highness," said the servant. "What would you like to wear in the meantime?"

My gaze traveled to the right, where shelves held countless pairs of the Fiend Prince's trousers, shirts, and doublets. I smiled at the servant. "I'll dress myself," I told her.

She left without protest. When I emerged from the closet, I was wearing a pair of the prince's lounge pants—probably loose on him, but nicely snug around my thighs and rear—paired with a silky embroidered shirt. I had combed out my hair, which fell below my waist, and I'd woven it into one long braid.

The Fiend Prince was sitting in the breakfast nook, the only part of his suite that had a window. He wore a dramatic outfit of black brocade with a high collar, satin ribbing, and blousy sleeves. When he saw me, a lump of egg fell from his mouth onto his thigh. A servant rushed forward, snatched the lump, and dabbed at his pants with a cloth.

"Wife." The prince cleared his throat. "What are you wearing?"

8

"You can call me Amarylla, you know," I said, seating myself primly across from the Fiend Prince.

"What would Her Highness like to eat?" stammered one of the servants. "We have ham, eggs, puff pastry, fruit tartlet, candied almonds, creamed wheat with sugar and berries—"

"Eggs and fruit tartlet, please." While they served me, I busied myself with spreading my cloth napkin across my lap and smoothing a crease in the tablecloth, looking anywhere but the Fiend Prince's eyes.

"Amarylla," he said.

My heart jumped. "What?"

"You said I could call you Amarylla. I was testing it out. I don't like it. It sounds like a poison."

"That's amaryllis, and yes, I was named for a beautiful toxic flower. What's your name?"

"You don't know?"

"Everyone here calls you 'Your Highness,' and to your enemies, you're 'the Fiend Prince.' But I'm your—" I nearly gagged on the word, but I forced it out— "your wife, and I should know what to call you."

"Ah." He nodded. "You want to have something to scream when we're making love."

At his words, I choked, and the chunk of ham I'd just swallowed stuck in my throat. I struggled to swallow it back down, but it was stuck. Frantically I beat at my own chest, unable to breathe or speak.

"Princess?" said a servant tentatively. "Are you unwell?"

The Fiend Prince lunged out of his chair and hauled me out of mine. Black spots were dancing before my eyes, thickening and swirling. He pulled my back against his chest, wedged his fist beneath my ribs, and capped his other hand over it. A quick jerking squeeze, and the stubborn chunk of ham dislodged, flying onto the tablecloth. I gasped, inhaling the blessed, blessed air.

He pressed both hands flat against my stomach, holding me against him for a second. "I believe I just saved your life."

Damn it. He did. Just when I didn't want to owe him anything else...

"Thank you," I gritted out.

One of his hands slid to my hip, then to my ass cheek, cupping it through the soft material of the lounge pants. "My clothes fit you well," he said.

I acted on pure instinct, born from years of training. My hand latched on his wrist, jerking it forward and twisting. In a split second, I had him on the ground with my bare foot pressed to his neck.

The click of a crossbow, and the threatening voice of a guard. "Release the prince at once."

"No, no," gasped the prince. "It's fine. She promised to show me that move—really, it's all right."

I recoiled, releasing his wrist and letting him up. I would have to be more careful. I was lucky the guards hadn't shot me instantly. And I had nearly blown our cover as the more-or-less-happy newlyweds.

"Sorry," I faked a giggle and curtsied to the frowning guard before resuming my place at the table.

"It's all right, Princess," said the Fiend Prince coolly. "As for the lifesaving bit, you can show me how grateful you are later. I have meetings this morning." He shoveled another bite into his mouth before striding out of the room. A couple servants stayed behind to tidy the suite, though it looked gloomily impeccable to me.

The day proved insufferably boring. No one appeared to take me to any training or exercise room, and all but one of the servants left. The remaining servant, who said her name was Sil, answered my questions about the palace and the kingdom with one-syllable words or obscure, annoying phrases like, "As it has always been," or "If it please Your Highness to think so," or "The Dreadlord's will is our guide." Her favorite phrase seemed to be "What a funny question," followed by a chuckle and no information at all. By mid-afternoon, I wanted to strangle her.

Finally the Fiend Prince stormed back into his suite, his pale features taut with anger and his eyes blazing. He dismissed the servant curtly and stalked into the washroom without a glance at me.

When he did not come out for several minutes, I edged close to the open archway and listened.

Absolute silence. What could he be doing?

Cautiously I peeked in.

He was sitting on the black marble step beside the big claw-footed tub, his face in his hands and his hair disheveled. A flicker of pity wavered in my heart.

"Did something happen?" I asked, and he started violently.

"Yes, something happened," he snapped. "I was *married* yesterday, and now I don't have a moment's peace or privacy, even in my own rooms! And my father won't move you to your own suite because he wants me to take every available opportunity to impregnate you. Which is what I am supposed to be doing right now. I was kicked out of a meeting, told to go and plow my wife again. Humiliating. I've been demoted from battle god to stud horse."

"So you were a warrior."

"As I told you."

"And something happened to make you—like this."

"Yes, like this—weak," he hissed. "Damaged. Worthless. And you don't care—healthy and strong as you are—enemy of my people, daughter of a greed-soaked nation—I can't stand to look at you. Get out. Get away from me. Go!"

He barked the orders so emphatically, with such ferocity in his eyes, that I left. I hated doing anything that looked like obeying him, but my presence was obviously salt in whatever wound was plaguing him.

I went and sat by the fire and read one chapter of a sort-of interesting book called "Customs and Conquests of the Northern Ranges." It didn't have much information about Terelaus itself, but a good deal about neighboring nations, and how they had fallen under the sway of the Dreadlord.

Eventually the Fiend Prince emerged from the bathroom and threw himself into a big chair near mine. He stretched out long, stick-thin, black-clad legs. By contrast, his boots looked comically large. "We'd better make some more sounds." He spoke as if nothing had happened between us, as if he hadn't broken down and shouted at me.

With a slap I shut my book. "All right then. Moan away. But don't complain about my sounds this time."

9

The Fiend Prince looked toward the door. "Anyone could walk in. We should position ourselves convincingly—here, you come and sit on my lap—"

"Definitely not."

"Then you lie on the couch and I'll get astride you."

"No."

"Fine. Then you hold onto the back of the chair, bend over, and I'll—"

"Gods, would you stop?" I clapped my hands over my ears. "I'll sit on your lap then."

"No, actually, that won't work—you're wearing pants. You see, this is why you should wear skirts—it's easy to hide what you're doing—or not doing—underneath them. If you had a dress on you could just sit on me and drape it over both of us, and anyone popping in would suspect that the most illicit things were happening beneath the voluminous fabric, when in reality, nothing would be happening at all."

"I'll take the pants off," I said, my face hot. "This shirt is long enough to hide the rest."

He nodded, so I unfastened the pants and slipped them off. It felt odd to be barelegged in front of him, and more so when I arranged myself astride his lap, facing him. The long silk shirt draped my thighs and rear, covering the fact that I was still wearing my underwear. Anyone walking in would think we were coupling, when instead, I was protected from such congress by a thin layer of soft material, and by the thicker fabric of his black pants.

My knees and shins pressed into the velvety cushion of the chair. I didn't know where to put my hands. And I was much too close to the Fiend Prince's pretty mouth. At this range, a sneaky glance told me his eyes were dark brown, nearly black.

His hands drifted to my hips, hovering but not quite touching. "If anyone comes in, start moving a little, up and down," he instructed quietly. "As if you're—"

"I get it," I snapped, keeping my face turned aside from his.

At that very moment, a man opened the bedroom door and leaned in. He didn't say anything, just looked at us. Immediately I shifted my hips, moving against the Fiend Prince's body and moaning faintly. With a satisfied expression, the man at the door nodded and ducked back out.

I leaned in to whisper to the prince. "He was definitely checking up on you."

"What did he look like?"

Briefly I described the man, and the prince nodded. "One of my father's favorite snoops." His hands settled on my waist, warm through the silk shirt. "We should make a few more sounds, just in case he's still listening."

"All right." I cleared my throat and gave a half-hearted groan.

The prince smiled, and his pelvis bucked suddenly upward, grinding against my center. "Oh," I gasped.

"There," he said. "Much more convincing." His hands on my waist pressed down, and he ground his hips again, humming deep in his throat. I bit my lips, fighting against the sound that wanted to escape me, because the friction felt *good*. It was all I could do not to writhe wildly against him.

"Let it out," he whispered. "Open your mouth."

The next time he moved, I let my lips fall apart and a little cry escaped me, a sound halfway between a yelp of pain and a startled gasp, except it was neither of those things. The Fiend Prince looked at me with malevolent satisfaction in his eyes. "You're a naughty little Princess at heart, aren't you?" he said softly.

Flushed and confused, with a strange liquid heat flaring at my core, I lurched off his lap and stumbled away from him. Now it was my turn to long for some privacy. I snatched my discarded pants and marched into the closet, burying myself in the dark behind a row of tailcoats.

I pulled the pants on, but not before experimentally touching my damp underwear. I wanted to keep touching, but the prince's voice slithered into the closet, somewhat muffled by layers of hanging fabric. "Princess, did I embarrass you? That wasn't my intention." But he sounded much too pleased with himself for it to be a genuine apology.

"I'm going to my study now," he said. "The servants will be back soon to dress you for the celebration tonight. We'll be expected to dance, to eat, to drink, to be charming. I hope you can manage that. If you behave in a satisfactory manner, as my bride, I'll see to it that you get your training and exercise space tomorrow."

His footsteps faded, and I shrank to the floor, pressing my fingers to my lips.

Why had I agreed to sit on his lap? Why had I let him hold my waist? Why had I let myself get carried away? This man wasn't kind. He was a killer, a battle-hardened warrior who had personally slain hundreds of my father's soldiers. Rumors claimed he rode to war in black armor studded with red gems—that he wielded a massive sword with a glowing scarlet blade, which drank the blood and souls of the people he killed. They said he hurled great whips and bolts of blazing magic across the battlefield.

Magic.

I hadn't seen him use magic at all—not a lick of it. And when his father suggested he sedate me, there was no mention of magical means of restraint. Surely if the Fiend Prince were able to wield magic, he could have used it to bend me to his will.

People with magic occasionally popped up in other lands, but Terelaus had an overabundance of magic-users. Many of their soldiers used minor magic—blasts of light, bolts of fire, crackling energy nets, that sort of thing. Others, like the sorcerer who'd brought me here, had much greater magical abilities, rarer and more refined.

Maybe the Fiend Prince's malady, whatever had rendered him "worthless," had to do with the loss of his magic. And if I could find out how he lost his power, maybe I could find out how to drain magic from every sorcerer and wielder in Terelaus.

If I could figure that out, maybe I would get to go home.

10

A few hours later, after a tornado of servants had spun around me awhile, I emerged in the white dress with the silvery swirls, which left my shoulders and cleavage on display. I'd been sponged, painted, bejeweled, and coiffed until I gleamed like the trophy I was. My long hair had been parted and tied into puffy sections, a tradition for Terelonian brides.

The Fiend Prince and I left his quarters together in silence, flanked by several guards who all kept their hands on their sword-hilts and eyed me with expressions hovering between awe and suspicion. News of my combat skills must have traveled through the Cursed Palace. I could not help but smirk with satisfaction at the thought.

As we walked, I tried to commit the route to memory. The sooner I learned the layout of this place, the better. The Fiend Prince had called the Cursed Palace "a maze," and I soon discovered why. We must have passed fifty different hallways, narrow passages, and twisty stairways hewn from rock. After the twentieth turn, I gave up trying to keep track of the rights and lefts.

The Fiend Prince leaned close to me. "You look disgruntled, dearest. Try to assume a slightly more docile expression. Remember, you've been pleasantly surprised by my stamina and sexual prowess, and now you're entirely content to be my bride."

"Of course," I said through a savage smile. "I'm the happiest of happy prisoners."

He threw me a warning glance. "Here we are. Remember what's at stake."

My training space. An exercise area just for me, where I could grow even stronger, strong enough to fight my way out of here. Except that no amount of fighting would get me past the magic-users of this land. To escape, I would need to know more about them, which meant I would need to earn trust, put everyone off their guard, convince them that I liked it here and that I wouldn't try to escape. I needed all of them, from the lowliest servant to the Dreadlord himself, to trust me.

I flashed the Fiend Prince my best smile—the one I used when I toured villages with my father or rode in the parade on holidays. A beautiful, practiced smile, one that lit up my face and showed every feature to best advantage.

The Fiend Prince's eyes widened, and his lips parted a bit. He was still staring at me when a guard murmured, "Your Highness? Are you ready?"

"What? Oh... yes." The Prince straightened his tailcoat. "Proceed."

The guard nodded and tapped on the doors in front of us. From beyond them I heard a herald's voice, "Announcing His Infernal Highness the Fiend Prince of Terelaus, Warrior of the Gods, Builder of Empires, and his bride the Princess Amarylla of Brintzia."

The doors parted, probably by magic—I could see no one touching them. I laid my hand on the Prince's proffered arm and we glided into the room beyond—a room scattered with strangers dressed in dark clothing. Other than the occasional jewel-toned cape, accessory, or headpiece, most of the crowd wore black.

"Is black your national color?" I whispered to the Prince.

"It would seem so," he replied, with a salacious smirk, as if we were whispering naughty secrets. For a moment I wondered what devilish things he might whisper to me if we really were enamored with each other. Looking at him now, at his fine features and flawless skin, I could not imagine what had made him so reluctant to remove his mask last night. Could there be some magical reason, or perhaps a cyclical plague that affected him at certain times? I'd never heard of such a thing, but then again, not much was known about Terelaus and its people, beyond their apparent yearning to conquer every nation that touched their current borders.

We both smiled and waved to the dour-faced courtiers we passed. Most of them watched me with narrowed eyes—displeased, curious, or suspicious—or perhaps all three at once. I had no doubt there were families of noble blood in the crowd who had hoped their own son or daughter might catch the Fiend Prince's eye and become a royal. And here I was, daughter of an enemy kingdom, taking that coveted place as the broodmare for Terelaus's prize stud.

Was I only a convenient bride, a political chess-piece that happened to become available at the right time? Or was there another reason why the Dreadlord had chosen a daughter-in-law from beyond his own borders?

Too many questions, and they all swirled behind my bright eyes and saccharine smile as I floated along at my new husband's side.

We approached the grand banquet table on the dais at the head of the room. The Dreadlord sat there, wearing a half-mask beneath which I glimpsed a hard, stubbled jaw and thin lips.

The Fiend Prince and I bowed and curtsied before him, then moved around the table and took our places at his right hand. Thankfully we did not have to sit immediately beside him—our chairs were set farther along the table, leaving a wide berth between us and the Dreadlord. I was immensely grateful for the distance. The Dreadlord cowed me with his very presence, and I did not enjoy feeling small and subdued.

The other guests all took their places at various tables throughout the room, and a low hum of conversation began. I could only imagine what the nobles might be saying about me and the Fiend Prince. My stomach tightened, my bowels spasming with nerves. When the servants brought out a thin creamy soup as the first course, I could barely sip it. I took a few of the small dry crackers that accompanied it, relishing the crunch and the hint of salt.

"Keep smiling at everyone," the Prince murmured. "I know looking pleasant is a terrible chore for you, but you must make a greater effort. To be honest, you look rather ill."

"I *feel* rather ill," I whispered back.

"Nerves." He nodded so companionably that I wanted to smack him and remind him that we were not friends. "I sometimes have them before a battle."

"You mean you get nervous before you go out to slaughter people and steal their land?" I said sweetly. "You poor darling."

He cast a baleful look at me, but he did not reply, because servants were delivering the next course—tender pink slices of meat on beds of greens. Once the servants had retreated again, he jabbed a piece of meat with his fork and said in an undertone, "My life is far less simple and barbaric than you believe, Princess."

11

I picked at the rest of the courses. Delicious though they looked, I was too anxious to eat much. I felt tense, drawn tight like the string of a crossbow. When a group of musicians at the other end of the chamber began to play, I let out a quick gasp of relief and seized the Prince's hand. "Let's dance."

He stared. "You want to dance? With me?"

"You said we would need to."

"Yes, but not until later in the evening."

"In my country, the royals always open the dance."

"Fine." The Fiend Prince beckoned to the herald, who stood by the wall, behind the Dreadlord's seat. When the man approached, the prince said, 'Please announce that in accordance with the customs of the Princess's homeland, she and I will begin the first dance."

The herald halted the musicians with a sharp gesture. Then he cleared his throat and made the proclamation, while the Fiend Prince led me around the table, off the dais, and into the middle of the room.

Why did I think dancing would make me feel better? Now I was truly the center of attention, the oddity for all eyes to fix upon. My fingers trembled in the Prince's hand.

"Losing your nerve already, wife?" He gave me an insolent smile that sent steel right into my bones.

"Just wondering if you're any good as a dancer," I said airily. "I'm about to put you to shame."

"Is that so?"

"I'm good at fighting," I told him. "And dancing is all about rhythm and footwork." Music flooded the space, swirling around us, merging with my blood and singing in my bones. Whatever they lacked in color, the Terelonians had good music with a seductive beat.

I circled the Fiend Prince slowly, then laced my right hand with his. His fingers slid, warm and supple, right into the sensitive notches between my own fingers. His left palm found my waist, and we began to dance, cautiously at first, with simple steps—and then, as he kept pace easily, with more complex steps, weaving a pattern across the glossy black floor. I glimpsed our reflection in its lake-smooth surface—a figure in a ghost-white gown, dancing with a skeletal black-clad wraith. Wilder we danced, faster we whirled—the prince whipped me around and pulled me against him, my back to his chest, his hands clasping my wrists. I broke his grip easily and twirled away, only to be recaptured as he quick-stepped after me.

More couples joined the dance, but I barely noticed them, so intent was I on my dance-fight with the Fiend Prince. Every intricate sequence of mine, he matched to perfection. His dark eyes mocked me, challenged me; his slim legs and lithe body mimicked every sway and swerve of mine, every arch and slither. I found myself testing more salacious moves just to watch him follow them, just to see how well he could synchronize himself to the melody and to my whims.

But he was breathing fast, and a hectic flush burned in his cheeks. The set of his mouth spoke of something beyond determination—it hinted of pain. I was pushing him beyond his physical limits, and he was too proud to say it.

I stepped in close, my breasts grazing the front of his fine tailcoat. Again I smelled his unique fragrance—licorice and myrrh, spices and darkness.

"Are you tired, sweet husband?" I murmured. "Shall I go a bit easier on you?"

"No," he growled.

"Are you certain?" I twirled away, but he yanked me back with a frenzied strength I did not expect.

"You may be stronger in body, for now," he hissed. "But I have the stronger will."

"Unlikely. And I think, strong will or no, you are nearing your physical limits. After just one dance, too. Such a pity. What were you saying earlier, about your stamina?"

He seethed at me. "Lower your voice."

"But my darling husband, I want everyone in Terelaus to know of your incredible stamina, and your prodigious length, and how deeply you satisfy me, your fortunate wife."

From the sidelong looks of several dancers, I was clearly overhead. My joint purpose, of feigning satisfaction with my marriage while embarrassing the prince at the same time, had been achieved. I gifted him with an angelic smile and whirled into his arms as the song ended. He embraced me a little too tightly, and with his mouth at my ear he said, "You think you've won, little wife. Wait until we return to my rooms. You will be thoroughly punished for your insolence toward me tonight."

Something dark crawled through his tone, and I shivered in his arms—partly from apprehension, and partly from a strange kind of anticipation. What punishment could he intend to inflict on me? Would he actually harm or torture me? Have me whipped, perhaps? He seemed too genteel for that, but he was the Fiend Prince, relentless warrior and slayer of countless soldiers, men and women. Perhaps he was not above bringing bodily harm to his rebellious wife. And since he knew I was strong enough to resist him, he would probably ask a sorcerer or his guards to do the job.

The next song began, a slow, sultry melody this time, meant for quiet swaying in the arms of a lover. The Fiend Prince gathered me close, my body pressed to his, and he smiled warmly, as if he truly cared for me. But I could see the daggers glinting unsheathed in his eyes.

12

By the end of the dance, the Fiend Prince's breath was labored, although he was taking pains to hide the fact. He dragged me to the front of the room for a farewell obeisance to his father, and then the herald made a hasty announcement of our sudden exit. As the Fiend Prince and I left the ballroom, I heard the Dreadlord's sonorous voice making some comment about newlyweds and their urges—and a chorus of titters followed his words. My cheeks heated, but a moment later I forgot my embarrassment, because the Fiend Prince was gripping my arm desperately, putting much of his weight on me.

I considered telling his guards of his predicament and asking them to help him along; but when I glanced at him, he looked so fiercely determined, so intensely, painfully proud—I couldn't betray that pride. So instead I shifted, moving my arm around his body, giving him the support he needed.

When we reached his room he dismissed the guards and servants curtly at the door, and I wound my other arm around him, too, giggling. "We can undress ourselves," I said, with a saucy wink, and they retreated quickly.

The instant the door closed, the Fiend Prince sagged against me, gasping. I knew that sound—not pleasure, but pain and exhaustion.

"Come this way, you skinny idiot." I hustled him toward the bed. "How are you still this heavy when you're so thin? I suppose it's your height. You're so damn tall—gods, it makes this a lot harder. Why couldn't I be married to a short little twig of a prince?"

"For stars' sake, shut up," he groaned.

"I think you mean, 'Thank you for your help, my beautiful and powerful wife. Please allow me the honor of setting you free and sending you home at the next available opportunity.' That's what you meant, isn't it?" I dumped him on the bed, clothes and all, and he lay there, panting, his cheeks still flushed with exertion. His dark hair clung to the film of sweat across his forehead.

"You shouldn't have danced so much." I fought the urge to scrape that damp hair back from his face. "But you were a passable partner."

"Passable?" he wheezed. "I suffered all that for *passable*?"

I turned my back to him. "Undo my buttons, if you have the strength for that tiny task. Otherwise I'll have to call the servants back in and they'll see you like this."

He moaned, but I felt him undoing the buttons, one by one. With each button released, my dress fell wider apart, baring more of my back to the cool air of the room. "You Terelonians like it a bit chilly, don't you?" I shivered.

"You could stoke the fire, add a log," he suggested, undoing another button. This time his fingertips grazed my skin.

"It must take so much wood to warm your kingdom every winter," I said. "How do you manage?"

"Our forests are carefully guarded and preserved," he said. "Else we'd have none left. We ration the firewood." He undid the last button. This one lay near the base of my spine, and when his fingers brushed my skin again, I couldn't suppress another shiver.

I slid off the bed quickly and faced him. "So your people suffer while you burn as many logs as you like? What do they do when they run out of wood?"

He looked at me, tousled dark hair and flushed cheeks and pain-bright eyes above that too-pretty mouth of his. "Body heat."

"Oh." I paused, suddenly conscious that I'd been about to slide the dress right off my shoulders, and that I'd forgotten I wore nothing underneath. The dress itself had enough structure that I'd been able to go without a corset.

"Close your eyes," I told the prince.

"And deprive myself of the only source of delight in my life at this moment? Not likely."

He meant it as a wry, defiant statement, but it touched something inside me and made me pity him more. This fallen prince, whatever he had once been, seemed miserable—emotionally as well as physically reduced. I knew first-hand how it felt to be overlooked, disappointed, treated as a commodity. I knew the strain of royal responsibility to a nation at war—perhaps not as keenly as my father had, or as this prince did, but still.

I turned my back to him and slid the dress off my shoulders, until I stood half-naked, dressed only in the hoops and petticoats of the gown. Carefully I unfastened the remaining layers and stripped down to my lace underthings. Then I went to the closet and fetched one of his tunics to serve as my nightshirt.

When I came back, the Fiend Prince eyed the bare length of my legs appreciatively. "If I had the strength to ravage you--"

"You wouldn't, and we both know it," I told him. "If you wanted to assault me you would have done it already. Though you have invaded nations, I suspect it's not in your nature to invade women in that way, no matter how great the temptation." I perched on the edge of the bed and began unfastening his coat, then his shirt.

"Undressing me, Princess?" His voice carried the faintest echo of his usual bravado.

"I can help you undress, or you can sleep in all this finery and ruin it. Your choice."

Grumbling, he dragged himself to a sitting position and helped me take off his garments, but the effort made him sweatier, and this time he grew deathly pale instead of flushed. When the upper clothes were off, I made him lie down while I undid the buttons of his pants.

His jaw was set tight, his hands curled into fists while my fingers eased each button out of its slot. Despite my care not to touch him more than necessary, his arousal was plain as I dragged the pants off him. From the way it tented his undershorts, he was rather impressively made, as I'd suspected from my earlier contact with that area.

"So flushed, Princess," he said. "But you've seen a man's parts before and had one inside you, yes? You claim not to be a virgin, yet you also claim not to know how a woman sounds when she is pleasured. A mystery, indeed." He broke off, out of breath, and closed his eyes, dragging the sheet over himself.

I climbed into the bed as well, careful to keep my distance. In the darkness of the room, confession seemed easier, almost necessary.

"Not such a mystery," I said quietly. "The boy I was with put himself in quickly, and finished quickly, and took no time for more."

"He took no time to please his princess?" The Fiend Prince sounded incredulous. "What an unworthy lout."

I chuckled a little. "Well. He was good-looking. I thought that meant the experience would be good, too. Clearly I was misinformed."

The Fiend Prince rolled onto his side, facing me. "Would you like to be better informed?"

13

The Prince's question hung in the chilly quiet, unanswered.

I clawed the sheet and blanket closer to my chin. The room was dark, but when I sneaked a look at the Prince, I could make out his browbone, the slope of his cheek, and the line of his nose in the distant glow from the fireplace. His eye glinted, half-concealed by locks of tumbled hair dislodged from its usual neat placement. He was safer to be around when he was polished, and dressed. This bare-chested, tousled version of him was far more dangerous, despite his weakened state.

"What do you propose?" I managed.

"A conversation," he murmured. "I have no energy for anything more."

A conversation couldn't hurt, could it? I was curious how my body was supposed to work, to know what I was supposed to do to get that height of pleasure so many people seemed to enjoy chasing. I'd had no mother to explain it, and when I had asked my maids back home, they had merely tittered and said it wasn't their place to tell me. I'd questioned my training partner Ashari too, but she told me she wasn't interested in such things and would rather not discuss them.

Here was someone willing to indulge my curiosity—someone with experience. And since he was my husband, the conversation wouldn't be inappropriate. Not that "appropriateness" ever stood in the way when there was something I really wanted.

"How—how would we begin such a conversation?" I asked.

"First of all, let me ask if you have ever explored yourself. Your nether regions, your private areas."

I pulled the sheet over my face. "Mmph."

"I cannot hear you, Princess."

"Yes, I have," I said grudgingly. "It felt nice enough, but not as good as I think it's supposed to feel. I've always gotten distracted or fallen asleep before I got much pleasure from it."

He laughed, thin and hoarse. "Then you're doing it wrong, I think. Or maybe you need something to look at. Some people think men are the only ones who like some visual stimulation, but that's not true. I've found that women appreciate a sensual sight just as heartily. And now we encounter a problem, because, as you've said, you don't find my body attractive. So the sight of me won't help you at all."

I chewed my lip, glad he could not see my face. I was probably red as a furnace. "I—I don't find you completely unappealing."

"Really? Well then—" He rolled onto his back again and threw the sheet off himself. His pale torso glistened faintly with sweat, and though he wasn't gifted with mounds of muscle, the lean cut of his chest, the lines of his ribs, and the concave plane of his stomach warmed my blood. Even the twisting map of his scars intrigued me. His hipbones jutted sharp, and the slope of his abdomen tapered invitingly toward the band of his undershorts. Judging from the lump beneath them, he wasn't as firmly erect as he'd been earlier.

"Like anything you see?" he asked. "How do you feel now?"

"I feel—" My heartbeat throbbed hard through my veins, pulsing in the space between my thighs.

"What if I take these off?" He tucked his thumbs into his waistband, easing the shorts down a bit lower. "What then?"

Tingling heat swelled in my lower belly, a warm wave of sensation I wasn't prepared for.

"Don't," I whispered. "I can't do this." I pressed my hand over my eyes.

"You can do anything you want," he said. "If you want to go to sleep, so be it. If you want to watch me touch myself, we can do that too."

"Watch you—" I gulped. Suddenly, desperately, I *wanted* to watch, to see what he would do. But when I peered at his face, I saw that his eyes were closing, dark lashes drifting to his cheeks. "You're not well. You should rest."

"Mm," was all he said in response. "I think I will sleep. Feel free to look at me all you want."

And I did look. I stared at him, even after his breath grew calm and slow. I decided I liked the crisp lines of his collarbones, the vulnerable softness of his mouth in sleep. I liked the neat corner of his jaw, and the way his dark hair swirled across his temple in frayed silky bits. I liked the tight buds of his nipples, and the fine bones of his hands, and the way his abdomen sucked in and lifted with every light breath.

I could kill him now, easily. I could insert the tip of a blade into that pale throat and release the red blood, or press a pillow to his face. He would not have the strength to resist me.

Frantically I searched my heart for the burning ache of vengeance, the desire to kill him. I could not find it. He had doused it thoroughly, sometime between our dance and this moment.

How had this man, barely more than a boy, killed so many of my people? Why had he slaughtered my father's soldiers, and ridden at the head of raiding parties that burned our border villages? I couldn't reconcile the two people—the warrior and the dancer—as one. Though as a warrior and dancer myself, perhaps it should not have surprised me that he could hold both identities at once.

A shiver coursed over my skin, and I curled in on myself, hoping I would warm up soon. The Fiend Prince lay exposed, goosebumps stippling his skin in the chilly air. After a moment I dragged the sheet and blankets over him as well, and as I did so I felt the faint warmth of his skin, a delicate temptation.

Gingerly I eased my body closer to him. And closer again. And just a tiny bit closer, until my arm was pressed to his. Just that bit of contact warmed me, and when he did not stir, I sighed, relaxing. Slowly my thoughts diffused into dark, silky warmth—heat and smooth skin and delicious comfort.

When I roused to consciousness again, I felt as if I had more limbs than usual. A weight on my waist, a solid thigh between mine.

My eyes flew open, and there were the Fiend Prince's nose, eyelashes, and cheekbones, a finger-space from mine. His eyes were closed.

A twitch of panic jarred my body, and he mumbled, frowning, pulling me tighter against him.

I froze, wincing. How was I to get out of this? A timepiece hung on the wall beyond his shoulder, far beyond the drape of the bed-curtain, and if I squinted I could read its markings. It was nearly morning—the servants would be coming soon with breakfast. Our interwoven position would certainly confirm our status as a happy couple. Perhaps I should stay like this a while. It wasn't so bad, after all, with his hair gliding like a silky breath across my forehead and his hand cupping my rear, squeezing lightly—

Wait a minute—

I wriggled, trying to shake off his fingers. "You bastard. You're awake."

14

The Fiend Prince squeezed my ass cheek a little harder. "What do you know… I *am* awake."

"Bastard," I hissed again, struggling to extricate myself.

He began moving away from me, and his thigh slid between mine, a rough unintentional caress against certain private places. I let out a small sound and my eyes flared with alarm, catching his gaze. We both froze, interlaced, tense and motionless. He swallowed, his lashes dipping as he eyed my mouth. "Your breath is terrible, Princess."

"So is yours, fiend." I pinched my lips together.

"We should go and tend to that, and to—other needs."

"There's only one bathroom."

"So we'll share."

"Not a chance," I said. "I'll go first."

"Be quick then, or I may have to piss into the fireplace."

"You disgust me."

"Tell me, do you often cuddle all night with people who disgust you?"

"Despicable monster," I hissed, wrenching myself away from him. "How many innocent men and women have you killed?"

I lunged out of the bed, not even caring that my makeshift nightshirt was hanging off one shoulder. As I marched around the bed on my way to the bathroom, the Fiend Prince sat up.

"War is a harsh taskmaster, Princess," he said quietly. "It brings death to the best of warriors."

"Then why not stop it? Why continue conquering all the lands around your kingdom? Why not be satisfied with what you have?"

"Our resources here in Terelaus are severely depleted."

I paused in the doorway, startled. "You mentioned a firewood shortage—"

"There's a shortage of *everything*. We are a nation worn threadbare, skeletal. The wars my father has waged ever since my birth have sapped our strength, reduced us to a war machine whose fuel is now running low. Why do I fight my father's battles?" He rose from the bed, tall and thin, a shadow of desperation. "I fight to end them, Princess. I keep hoping that with one more conquest we will have what we need, and he will be satisfied, and we can settle into peace and focus on renewing our lands. But he is never satisfied. Not with our conquests, not with his own power, and not with me."

He stalked to the fireplace, bracing a palm against the mantel. "Get on with your business, Princess."

I went to the bathroom and took care of my needs as quickly as I could. When I came out again, with much sweeter breath, he took his turn, while I sat in one of the plush chairs and pondered what he had said.

He reappeared, still wearing only the undershorts, and I motioned for him to come over.

"What resources do your people lack?" I asked.

"Everything." He sank into a nearby chair. "We've conscripted nearly every man and woman over fourteen, so there's no one left to build families. Birth rates have dropped to nearly nothing—we'll have no next generation at this rate. Our work force is stretched far too thin, and we've got no one to run the farms. Our growth season is short as it is, you see, and when we don't take full advantage of it, the food runs out. Right now all that's keeping my people alive is the tax of food and goods we collect from the neighboring kingdoms we've conquered. But they won't be able to support us indefinitely."

"I had no idea," I said faintly. "Terelaus seems so strong, so powerful. My people in Brintzia think your kingdom is indomitable, irresistible."

"It's all a carefully designed shell, crafted to inspire terror. An impressive shell, but it's only a matter of time before it cracks," he replied. "And still my father wants to conquer more, and rule more, and still he keeps seeking the—"

He broke off suddenly, looking away from me.

"Keeps seeking what?"

"Nothing."

"Don't lie to me. You don't do it well."

"That's a good thing, right? I'm an honest soul." He smiled brightly.

"You're not charming your way out of this. What is this resource your father is looking for? I can tell you whether or not my country has any of it. Might save the Dreadlord some time."

"This is not a question easily answered." He sighed. "And what he seeks is a secret, closely guarded. I can't tell you, because you're not one of us."

"Thank the stars for that." I narrowed my eyes, watching him as he got up to stoke the fire.

I'd gotten close to something important; I could feel it. This thing the Dreadlord sought—it was the reason for his rabid efforts to build an empire, to conquer anyone and everyone around Terelaus. What could it be? Gold? Jewels? Some precious mineral?

Maybe it had to do with magic. But no, that didn't make sense. Terelaus had ample magic, while the surrounding kingdoms had little or none at all.

I had to make the Fiend Prince explain. I had to force him or persuade him to tell me what his father wanted. I could beat it out of him, but that would be difficult to accomplish here, with guards just outside the door and servants liable to pop in at any moment. Besides, I wasn't sure I had the strength of will to hurt the Prince, even if he was an obnoxious prick.

Once, months ago, I'd heard a cook in my father's palace talking about how she persuaded her husband to buy her things by doing him 'special favors.' I didn't hear the whole conversation, but I did hear enough to know it involved her mouth on that male part of him—something I'd never done for the stable boy.

Was I so desperate to know the Prince's secret that I would do such a thing for him? In my current position, I had little else to trade. And despite the Prince's claim that he didn't like women who were stronger than him, I felt sure he'd react to my attentions. He'd gotten excited when I unbuttoned his trousers last night, and he'd fondled my ass this morning.

"If you'll tell me what your father is looking for," I said, "I will do something for you in return."

"Hm?" he said absently. "What will you do? Teach me how to dance like a possessed eel? How to snuggle with my mortal enemies? How to lace a corset?"

"No," I snarled. Licking my dry lips, heart pounding, I rose and walked up behind him. I slid my hand past his waist, down to his crotch, and stroked gently. "I will let you put this in my mouth."

15

The Fiend Prince sucked in a harsh breath and knocked my hand away from his crotch, whirling to face me with a look of utter disgust on his face. "I won't exchange information for pleasure," he said. "I don't pay anyone for sexual attentions, least of all you. You are my wife, not a whore. You should have more self-respect."

And of course the servants chose that very moment to walk in with the breakfast trays. I was fairly sure they'd heard him say, "You are my wife, not a whore," and so on.

The Fiend Prince went white and gritted his teeth. I could tell he didn't know what to say, how to fix what they'd overheard to make it work with the charade we were presenting to everyone else in the palace.

"My self-respect means nothing compared to your pleasure, Illustrious Prince of Darkness," I said quickly. "You don't want to ask this of me, and this brusque refusal is really your kindness, trying to spare my dignity—but I have no dignity where you're concerned. I want none." I moved closer to him, aligning my body with his, tilting my face up. "Let me do this for you."

His pupils dilated, and his chest lifted against mine. "Maybe after breakfast, dearest," he said, loudly enough for the words to carry. "See, the servants are here. We must curtail our passion in their presence."

"We can leave, Your Highness," one servant said. Her cheeks were scarlet. The other servant, a man, set down his tray hastily and hurried from the room without being dismissed.

"Come back in half an hour," the Prince called after them.

When the door closed, he backed away from me, his eyes dark with admiration and something else, something hotter. "You ingenious vixen."

I smiled. "Quick thinking is my specialty."

"An admirable quality in a queen. As are your fighting skills, your humor, your strength, your intelligence, your beauty—" He stopped, puckering his lips.

Curse my foolish heart for fluttering, and for sending a fresh wave of blood into my cheeks. "That's quite a list of compliments," I said. "Did you forget no one is listening?"

"*You* are listening," he replied. "And I believe you could do with a few compliments. Your father clearly did not value you enough. He should never have sent such a treasure to my father. The Dreadlord respects no one, and gave you to me as a broodmare, little knowing how much I—how much you were really worth."

My cheeks flamed hotter. "And how much am I worth?" I seethed. "What price would the Fiend Prince pay for me? Two kingdoms' ransom? Three?"

"You are finding offense where there is none intended," he said softly. "But to answer your question—I would pay everything, and nothing at all."

His fingers drifted along the slope of my neck, and his thumb brushed the tender skin below my earlobe. His hand slid to my nape, cupping it. Caution flared through my body because even a man of his lesser strength could snap my spine easily with that grip—yet it wasn't a grip after all, but a warm and gentle caress. I tilted my head back without thinking, tipping my mouth up as his descended.

The door of his suite burst open, and in glided the sorcerer who had brought me to the Cursed Palace. He wore elaborately styled purple robes, and his unmasked visage had all the softness of a spiked iron mace. Two guards accompanied him. "Your Highness, as soon as you have breakfasted, the Dreadlord requires you. There is an uprising in Purnyal, and your aid is needed to quell it."

An uprising? And the Prince was needed to quell it? But last night he'd been shaking, sweating, weak as a lamb. How could he possibly be expected to fight? It didn't make sense for the Dreadlord to send his son, frail as I knew him to be, to the battlefield.

I glared at the sorcerer. "The Prince isn't well. He—"

"I'm perfectly fine," the Prince interrupted. "I will go to the Dreadlord at once. I have prepared a special room for my wife's enjoyment—see that she is escorted there during my absence, whenever she likes. And give her whatever she wants."

He strode away from me, snatched a sausage roll from a breakfast tray, and disappeared into the closet to dress. I plopped into a chair and took a sweet roll and some bacon, gnawing both while eyeing the sorcerer with all the malevolence I could muster. He couldn't touch me with magic now, not when I was so obviously in the Fiend Prince's good graces.

A few minutes later the Prince swept out of the room with barely a glance at me, and the sorcerer followed him. The two guards remained, presumably to escort me when I was ready to visit my new room.

As soon as I had finished eating, I braided my hair, dressed in more of the Prince's loose, comfortable clothing, and went with the guards, following them through the maze-like passages of the Cursed Palace to a pair of glossy red doors. The guards turned aside, their backs to the wall, flanking the entrance. "The room, Your Highness," said one of them.

I pushed the handle and stepped inside, letting the door fall shut at my back.

The room stretched out before me, what seemed like miles of padded mats, leather-covered hanging bags, beams, bars—everything I could want or imagine pertaining to exercise and training. On one wall, a bracket contained blunted swords, staffs, and knives for practice. Along the opposite wall was a clear track with a target at the far end—a range for shooting. Practice bows and arrows were set up nearby.

Guilt seeped into my soul along with a rush of gratitude—because even though I loved this space, and I was awed by the obvious care and thought of the one who planned it, I recognized that my wishes had taken valuable time and resources away from the people of Terelaus.

What were they like, the actual people? Not the dull noble drones I witnessed at the royal dinner, or the guards who tramped the halls of the Cursed Palace—but the *people*, the ones forced to fight and die for the Dreadlord, the ones working themselves to the bone to keep the country running while their loved ones were at war. What were *those* people like?

Did they have an advocate? It didn't seem so. The Fiend Prince seemed to weave between desperation and a sort of feigned indifference. He kept up with his duties, but barely, and he seemed to lack the energy to push for any real change.

More than that, he seemed frightened of his father. Who wouldn't be, with a father called "the Dreadlord," one who waged incessant war and viewed his own son as either a prizefighter or royal breeding stock?

I mulled over those questions while I beat against the training dummies, and dashed across the beams, and leaped and somersaulted along the mats. After a while I grew tired of training alone and pulled one of the guards into the room with me. He seemed uncertain about battling the Crown Princess, but I spurred him on, encouraging him and battering him by turns until he began to fight in earnest. Once I had beaten him soundly, I took on the other guard.

How it happened, I wasn't sure, but a third guard replaced the second, and before long an entire group of the Cursed Palace guard had assembled along the fringes of the room. I was in my element, slicked with sweat, my braid whipping with every feint and parry, my feet solidly planted, and the good staff in my hands trouncing every guard who came up against me. Meanwhile the guards cheered me and their companions by turns, calling out bets and making jokes.

I was on my seventh guard, a stout woman with arms the size of my thighs, when the jovial shouts and barbed teasing of the guards faded to silence. With a clank and a rumble, they all sank to one knee, and the masked figure of the Dreadlord himself entered the room.

16

The woman I was fighting stumbled back and knelt clumsily, collecting her helmet and jamming it back onto her head.

I wiped my forehead with my wrist and stayed erect, facing the Dreadlord for a few seconds longer than the rest before I finally knelt. A small defiance, all I dared risk at the moment.

The Dreadlord paced in a half circle around me. Because of the mask and hood he wore, I couldn't tell if he was actually looking at me.

"Crown Princess," he said in his sonorous voice. "You have a warrior's skill."

"Yes, Dreadlord," I answered.

"Tell me, have you taken any blows to the stomach?"

I frowned, confused. "No, Dreadlord."

"Good. I would hate for the womb that will carry my son's heir to be damaged." His hand closed on the staff I held, and he jerked it away. "From this day forth, no one is to spar with the Crown Princess," he said. "She is not here to fight."

My fingers and lips trembled, but I gritted my teeth and pushed words between them. "Why *am* I here, Your Majesty?"

"What?"

"Surely you have other *wombs* equally worthy of carrying your son's heir—more worthy, in fact. Women of your own people who would count it a privilege. Why me?"

"You question my reasons?"

"Yes, Dreadlord. I do."

He wrapped a metal-gloved hand under my chin, clutching my jaw so tightly I nearly whimpered with pain. "You are here because I want your kingdom to bear unflinching loyalty to my throne. Because I want your father to know that his grandchildren live in the Cursed Palace under my dominance, and at my mercy. Because I want all nations to fear me, to know that I will take their sons and daughters whenever I please. Because, my dear, I have the power. I own your body, and the bodies of everyone else in my empire. You may have softened my son's mind with your wiles, you may have tricked him into some puppyish affection, but you will never outwit me. You will fear me, and submit to my will, as they all do."

The Dreadlord stepped back. "Take the Crown Princess to the whipping room. Use the Squid, ten lashes."

No one moved for a moment, until he said, in a deathly tone, "*Now.* And sop up some of her blood with a cloth, so I can send it to her father. He should know what happens to insolent princesses within my walls."

Two guards approached me tentatively, clearly expecting resistance—but I was weary from fighting, weak with the shock of the Dreadlord's pronouncement. I did not struggle. I was afraid any further defiance might worsen the punishment.

But I couldn't help murmuring, "I thought you were worried about my health."

The Dreadlord paused on his way out of the room. "We only need certain parts of you, my dear," he said. "You would do well to remember that."

When he was gone, the guards drew me along the corridors of the palace and down three flights of steps, to a long room whose stone floor bore patches of dark brown—the stains of old blood. A heavy-set woman was working over a screaming man, drawing out his fingernails one by one with a pair of beak-nosed tongs.

The guard on my left cleared her throat and spoke. "We bring you the Crown Princess, Haneia. By the order of the Dreadlord. Ten lashes with the Squid."

The big woman stumped over and leaned close to me. She was chewing a wad of something herbal and strong-smelling, and her teeth were spotted brown from the juice of it. "The Crown Princess, eh? I expected to see you here sooner, love. Thought I'd be having to chastise you for resisting the joys of the marital bed." She snorted a laugh. "But it seems you like your marital bed well enough, eh? Got a good one, has he? Knows how to get you juiced up and slip it in easy?"

The guard cleared her throat again. "Mind how you speak of the Fiend Prince."

"All right, all right. Don't get your skivvies in a twist. Strip her down and latch her in over there." She gestured to a post with manacles attached to it, one of the less frightening-looking stations in the room.

I'd never been in a torture chamber. I knew my father had a few—occasionally he needed information from spies and traitors; but he rarely ordered such torment, and he had never made me set foot in one of those places.

Now I was to be *whipped*—I who had never been punished physically in my life, except for on the training ground. And being bruised or battered during a fight was different from the pain that lay ahead of me.

The guard on my left gathered the hem of my shirt in her hands. She looked me in the eyes through the slots of her helmet. "My apologies, Princess," she whispered.

"You know the Fiend Prince wouldn't allow this," I whispered back.

"He wouldn't have a choice." Her voice was barely a breath. "None of us do."

A spark of rebellion flamed inside me. "But maybe *all* of you do. Together."

Her hands stilled for a second before she drew my shirt off. I wore a light corset beneath, and she unlaced that as well, removing it carefully, respectfully. She gestured for me to kneel so they could lock my hands into the restraints that hung from the whipping post.

"Your name?" I asked, as she closed the bands around my wrists.

"So you can ask the Fiend Prince to kill me later?"

"No. So I can remember you for your kindness."

"Betta."

"Betta," I repeated. "I'm Amarylla."

She bent her helmet in acknowledgement and backed away, along with the other guard.

The big woman approached me, trailing a fringe of whipcords across her palm. All the strands were bound to a thick handle.

"All right then, little princess," said the woman. "Let me introduce you to the Squid." She dangled it before my face. "Sixteen cute little braids of devil's reed, woven with razor-sharp shards of crystal. Tickles you real good."

She chuckled and moved around behind me as I knelt, half-naked, my spine bowed and my skin quivering with terrified expectation.

17

At the first blow, I bit my lip until it bled. I had never felt such a widespread burst of pain across my skin.

After the third blow, I gave up trying not to scream, and I shrieked aloud.

"There it is," said the whip-woman, and she groaned softly with obscene pleasure. "Sweet, sweet sounds. The young voices are always the purest. Come on, love, give me another good one."

"Damn you—" And then I screamed again as the lash clawed savagely across my back.

The whip-woman began to hum low in her throat while she beat me.

Five.

I yelled, wrenched at the manacles in agonized fury. I was going to kill that horrible woman, first chance I got—

Six.

I was shaking, my breasts quivering loose, my stomach sucking concave with my frantic breaths. My long braid swung and jerked with every blow.

Seven.

When the Fiend Prince returned, I would tell him exactly what I thought of his father—

Eight.

My stomach revolted, nausea building as the pain surged. I swallowed back the bile and braced myself—

Nine.

I hung by my arms, sagging limp, scarcely able to see through the blur of tears.

Ten.

Pain, incandescent, all-consuming.

Hands found my wrists, unfastening the shackles. Helping me up, wrapping me in some sort of cloth, and I screamed again, trembling at the contact of the cloth against my raw wounds.

"Have her hold it against her chest," muttered the guard Betta. The cloth left my back, and I clutched it to my breasts while the two guards hustled me back to the Fiend Prince's suite, nearly carrying me up the steps. Dizzily I collapsed on my stomach across the Prince's bed.

"Call one of the sorcerers to heal her," Betta ordered.

"We have no such orders from the Dreadlord," responded the other guard.

"If she's not healed, these will scar, and the Fiend Prince will be displeased," Betta snapped. "Do you want to endure his wrath? I don't."

"I'll ask about it." Footsteps receded, and Betta directed a couple of the servants to attend me. They dragged me upright again while I squealed with pain, and they stripped me down and wiped the sweat and blood from my body. I was put back to bed without a stitch of clothing, and my wounds were smeared with a cooling ointment.

This was the lowest point in my life. Whipped and thrown naked onto the bed of the man I'd been forced to marry. I had never felt so truly, terribly helpless. Consciousness receded and resurfaced until I wasn't sure how long I had dozed. No one came to heal me. Maybe the Dreadlord had forbidden it. My reality blurred and sharpened, synchronized with the agony of my flayed skin.

In the swirl of a dark dream I realized that someone was in the room—I could feel a presence. A servant, probably, checking on the Fiend Prince's tattered bride. Groggily I blinked awake, and found an expanse of glossy, rippling abdominal muscles at my eye level, along with a twisted scar that I recognized. Slowly I lifted my gaze higher, up to mounded pectorals, swelling biceps, massive shoulders, a thick neck corded with muscle. And at the top, a leering demon mask.

I'd seen that mask before. The mask of the Fiend Prince.

My pain-addled mind raced frantically. Did he have a double? A duplicate who fought his battles for him? No, that made no sense. Maybe others in the palace wore similar masks? Maybe—

"I've sent for a healer," he said, and there was no mistaking that youthful male voice, despite the fact that it was a bit deeper and darker than usual, colored with pity and rage. "My father refuses to let you use one of the palace sorcerers, but I know of other options."

I tried to scoot away from him and ended up whimpering pitifully instead. Closing my eyes, I tightened my lips until the pain lessened, and then I spoke. "What's going on? Are you the Fiend Prince's well-muscled twin?"

"No, nothing like that."

"How are you back so quickly? And how did you turn into a glorious hulking god-warrior?"

A breathy laugh echoed behind the mask. "High praise, Princess. I'm back because when you have a sorcerer who can transport you anywhere by magic, getting to and from the battlefront is a moment's work. I returned a few minutes ago—I took a little time for a wash because I didn't want to drip blood everywhere."

"Blood?"

His throat bobbed as he swallowed. "Not mine."

"Oh." I winced. "You didn't answer my other question. How did you change from what you were, into *this*?"

The gust of a sigh issued from the mask's sneering grin. "My father wouldn't want me to explain, but after what he's done to you in my absence, I'm feeling rebellious. So I'll tell you part of the story."

He knelt beside the bed, laying those sinewy arms across the edge of the mattress, looking into my eyes. "Back in your kingdom, you knew me as the Fiend Prince, yes? A powerful warrior who wielded great magic?"

"Yes," I replied. "My father's soldiers tell stories of how you charge their ranks, bearing an enormous scarlet sword that drinks souls. They say you wield bolts and whips of fire."

"All true. At least, it was. I was born with extraordinary natural magic. And I was as powerful a warrior as I was a sorcerer. Until I lost it all, through a terrible accident. The accident is something I can't tell you about—not yet. Let's just say that it left me without my magic, and sucked away my strength. I was devastated, but a little relieved, I suppose. I thought my condition might be an excuse, that I might be able to avoid killing for my father anymore. But the Dreadlord wanted his sorcerer and his warrior back, so he insisted I use something else to restore my abilities."

Shock and dread coiled in my gut. "What substance could give someone muscles and magic?" I whispered.

"I can't tell you that either."

"Because you don't trust me." I laughed faintly. "Who am I going to tell?"

"I just—I can't yield that information yet."

"Fine. Suit yourself." I averted my eyes from his fiendish mask. "So you consume this mysterious substance to make yourself powerful?"

"I only consume it when the Dreadlord needs me to appear in battle, or to rout some insurgents in one of his territories. The effect lasts a limited time. It consumes my body and my energy, and the recovery phase afterward is painful, more difficult each time. But, it allows me to look like this." He indicated his splendid physique. "For a little while, I get to feel like myself again."

"Why the mask though?"

Silence followed my question, and then he said, "There's a physical toll, a price to be paid, and it shows on my face."

18

"This 'price to be paid'—how does it manifest?" I asked, peering harder at the Prince's mask.

"How are you still this curious when your back has been ripped open?" His voice cracked with emotion. "I can hardly look at you."

"Then don't," I hissed.

"It's not that the sight of you disgusts me," he amended quickly. "It hurts me that you're in such agony. Do you want a stiff drink, maybe a tonic? Something to numb the pain and help you sleep until the healer arrives?"

"You think I don't see how you've skillfully avoided my question, Fiend Prince?" I retorted. "Tell me how you lost your magic, and what you've been doing to restore it, and what happens to your face! And while you're at it, tell me why you keep taking this substance to restore yourself, when it obviously isn't good for you and leaves you thin and weak!"

"I do it because I must." His voice was toneless, despairing. "Because the Dreadlord requires it. Even if it eats me alive and brings me down to an early grave, he will continue to require it."

"That's why he's so eager for you to father children," I gasped. "He's hoping they'll inherit the strength and the magic you lost. He wants to use them, like he has used you."

The Fiend Prince bowed his head slightly. "And he wants me to hurry up and accomplish the task of creating heirs, because—"

He didn't finish the sentence, but I grasped the meaning well enough.

The Fiend Prince was going to die. He would die young, a broken weapon in his father's hand, a blade worn down to nearly nothing. Whatever substance he was consuming to temporarily restore his strength and his magic was ruining his health—killing him. And for what? To feed his father's insatiable appetite for war and conquest?

I tried to sit up, but pain bit through my torn muscles and I only accomplished an infuriated wriggle. The sheet that was draped across my lower body slid lower; I could feel the cool waft of air across part of my backside.

"I won't let this happen to you," I panted. "I won't let that horrible man grind you to powder."

"No one resists him," replied the Prince. "You learned that quite painfully today."

"I only asked why he chose me to be your bride."

"Ah, but you see, the Dreadlord does not like questions," said the Prince wryly. "They betray independent thought, and lead to tricky things like the exercise of free will, which in turn leads to rebellion. He couldn't let your challenge pass. He doesn't let even the smallest hints of defiance or disagreement slip by without severe repercussions."

I clenched my teeth against the rising anger and a fresh twist of pain. "Are you making excuses for him?"

"Never. I am only explaining how careful you must be if you want to survive here. I would have warned you how you should deal with him—but I never thought he would seek you out."

"I hope he never does again." I tried to move carefully, just to shift my head to a fresh spot, and fire lanced across my back. I smothered my cry in the pillow.

"What can I do?" said the Prince in a pained voice. "How can I help?"

I blinked away tears and turned my face back to him. "You have magic right now, yes?"

"Yes. I would heal you if I could, but my brand of magic is for creating wounds, not repairing them."

"Distract me then. Show me some magic. As long as it won't make your condition worse."

"That ship has already sailed," he said. "Are you sure you want to see this?"

"Are you going to deny your wife's request after she's been whipped half to death?"

"I wouldn't dream of it." He straightened to his full height, squaring his newly broadened shoulders. I couldn't help ogling him—he was magnificent, all curves and cuts of muscle, glowing with apparent health. He turned his palms up and crooked his fingers, and white lightning crackled and snapped, connecting them. Red sparks popped and sizzling along those lines of white. The Prince made a motion as if he were running his hand along a rope, and a whip of dazzling red fire appeared, lashing through the air of the room. When he flicked it, the tip sliced a bit of the bedcurtain, leaving it charred and flaking.

I startled and cringed back. "I've seen enough whips today."

He compacted the whip instantly, smashed it to a red orb in his hands and then ground it out to nothing. "I'm sorry. I'm so sorry, I didn't think."

"It's all right." I hauled in air, trying to get control of my panicked breathing. "I did ask for a demonstration."

"Damned healer, where is he?" snarled the Prince. "I'm ordering you a drink."

"All right, yes," I relented, gasping. "Yes, a drink. A very strong drink, please."

I heard him speaking to someone at the door of the suite, and then he returned, crouching by the bed. His fingers grazed my temple, brushing aside strands of my hair that had worked loose from the braid. The gentle touch was a strange contrast with the hideous, mocking mask.

"Please take the mask off," I whispered.

"You'll vomit if I do," he whispered back.

"It's that bad?"

"Yes."

"Why does it only affect your face and not the rest of you?"

"It has to do with the energy centers of the body," he replied. "Different kinds of magic are centered in different areas. My center is in my head, my mind—the center of my forehead, specifically. So the most visible side effects are in that area. Others have to cover their stomach, or heart, or loins—"

"Wait, others?" I exclaimed. "Other people in Terelaus take this substance, too? The one that grants magical and physical power?"

He cursed softly.

Ha. The Fiend Prince let something important slip.

19

My oh-so-secretive husband had accidentally informed me that he was not the only one taking the mystery substance to make himself strong and magical. And my new knowledge had massive implications.

"That's how your armies are so powerful," I said eagerly. "That's why Terelaus has so many more magic wielders than other regions and nations. You've found something that gives normal humans magical abilities—temporarily, and at great cost, but still." I twitched, longing to close my hands around his neck and force the rest of the truth out of him. "I will discover your secrets, Fiend Prince."

He swore again. "You cannot tell anyone that you figured this out."

I gave him the prettiest smile I could muster. "Of course not, husband."

At that word, a low exhale issued from him. My smile melted away. Why should that simple, common term make him sigh like that, and why did I feel as if a newborn star were expanding inside my chest?

Slowly, tentatively, the Fiend Prince reached for my face again, tracing the delicate arch of my browbone, the curve of my cheek down to my chin. Then, with one fingertip, he stroked my lips.

I could barely breathe. His fingers were slightly thicker than they had been—not quite so elegantly breakable. I parted my lips under his touch and took the end of his finger between my teeth. When I closed my lips instinctively, he inhaled, slow and unsteady. He tasted warm, and salty.

What was I doing? I pulled back, letting the digit slip from my mouth.

"I'm sorry," I said. "I don't know why I did that. I—for a moment I forgot about the pain."

"Did you now," he said softly.

A door opened, and a servant approached with the drink the Fiend Prince had ordered, along with a narrow metal tube through which I could sip it without lifting my head. When the servant left, the Prince held the cup and the tube for me. "It's only wine," he said. "I didn't want anything that would sear your throat and make you cough."

I sipped gratefully, the liquid sliding warm along my throat.

We sat there a long time, without talking of any secrets, while he gave me wine now and then until I began to feel much less pain, and a general muzzy warmth.

"You have a lovely mouth," he said after I had sipped again.

"So do you." Weariness and wine made me more blunt than usual. "The first time I saw you, I thought you had the prettiest mouth I'd ever seen on a man. Just the loveliest lips that ever existed."

"Is that so? I thought the same thing about your breasts."

"Crude bastard." I shoved away the cup of wine.

"Why? Why is admiring your breasts any more vulgar than admiring your mouth?"

"Because—" I blinked, trying to formulate a clear answer through the wine-haze. I didn't drink often, and when I did the liquor affected me strongly. "Because breasts are *breasts*," I told him sagely. "They are *private*."

"Are they indeed? You know I can see a generous portion of one right now. Just the side, since you're on your stomach, but still. You're not wearing much, Princess. Want me to help you into some clothes?"

"Gods' bones, no." I shuddered. "That would hurt."

"Just some pants then."

"No, because if I get up you will see me." I lifted my eyebrows very high. "*All* of me."

"I promise to behave," he said. "Or I can call the servants if that would make you more comfortable."

"No, no servants. Dull, curious things full of eyes, they are. But I should probably get up." I sighed. "I need to piss. Stupid wine." Tears welled in the corners of my eyes. "It's going to hurt when I get up, isn't it?"

"Yes, love," he said quietly. "It is. I'm so sorry. I can't believe he did this to you. I will speak to him. It won't happen again."

"But it might," I whispered. "You can't stop him. You can't protect me, because you're afraid of him. And I can't protect myself, because he has too many soldiers and sorcerers. If it was just him, alone, I'd kick his lordly ass."

The Fiend Prince laughed, a glorious masculine sound that rippled inside me. A soft tickling sensation passed between my legs, tightening my lower belly.

"Do that again," I said.

"Do what?"

"Laugh."

He did, a light indulgent chuckle at my silliness, and the trickle of sensation grew stronger. Its presence took a little more of my pain away.

"Let me help you up," said the Fiend Prince. "I promise I won't look at you. I'll close my eyes."

"And I should trust the word of my mortal enemy?"

"Do you really think of me as your enemy?" The quiet ache in his voice spurred a flutter in my heart. "I suppose you would, after today's travesty."

"You don't trust me either," I pointed out.

"No," he admitted. "But I want to."

"Then let's test each other. I will close my eyes, and you'll remove your mask. You close your eyes and help me up. We'll both keep our eyes shut the whole time." My wine-addled brain suspected some flaw in that plan, but I couldn't think what it was. "Agreed?"

"You won't look?" he said tightly. "Because if you look, I'll know. You won't be able to keep quiet about it."

"I won't look at you, if you promise not to look at me."

"The sightless guiding the sightless. What could go wrong?" he muttered. "Very well. Close your eyes, and do not open them at the risk of losing my trust forever."

I pinned my eyes shut and listened to the sound of buckles and straps being undone, of something metallic being set on a side table. "There. My mask is off," he said. "And now I'm closing my eyes. Here's my hand." He touched my shoulder. "I'll help you get up. Not too slowly, or that will make it worse. Better to do it quickly. Ready? Now!"

20

Despite the wine, the ointment, and the arousal I had felt, my skin screamed when I rose up, and I screamed with it, swaying against the Fiend Prince. He almost closed his arms around me, but he pulled back his hands before they touched the sticky lash wounds across my back. Instead he cupped my shoulders, rubbing my upper arms soothingly.

When the first shock of pain eased a little, I realized that he was bare-chested, and I was entirely naked, my breasts squished against him, my hot skin seamed to his. He felt—delicious. Smooth and sleek and warm, a silky mountain of muscle.

"Are your eyes still closed?" I whispered.

"Yes, for all the good it's doing." He gave a ragged laugh. "Yours?"

"Shut tight."

"All right. To the bathroom, then. Slowly. I've got you."

Every step pulled at the wounds on my back, and I couldn't help whimpering aloud.

The Fiend Prince cursed savagely. "Where is that damn healer?"

"Your father probably intercepted him."

"Perhaps. He may want you to suffer for a night before he relents. But I will make sure someone heals you before those wounds become scars."

"Is that what you care about? Preserving my flawless flesh?" Maybe he cared so much because his own flesh had been torn and twisted.

"Your back is beautiful." The admission, in his quiet voice, so close to my ear—it made my insides swirl and twist delightfully. "You gave me a fine view of it the other night when you took off your dress. But it would be just as lovely with scars. My concern is for you, Princess."

We shuffled along, with barely any space between us. The tips of my breasts kept brushing against him as he guided me. I risked a flare of pain to wrap one of my arms across my chest; but it hurt too much, and I had to settle for keeping a little more distance, gripping the Prince's biceps while he held my upper arms.

"Are we moving the right way?"

"I know this room well," he said. "We are perfectly on target to reach the—ow!" A jarring impact slammed from his body through mine. He'd bumped into something. I yelped as my wounds flexed.

"On target, are we?" I snapped.

"Sorry. Here, this is the entrance."

Awkwardly he steered me in the right direction and gave me a little clumsy assistance with seating myself and getting up again after I'd done my business. My face was a furnace of shame. I'd had servants to help me with mundane tasks before, when I was sick or injured from training—but this was different. It was achingly intimate, and I felt exposed in a way I hadn't before. What if he didn't keep his eyes shut? What if he was looking at my whole body at this very moment while I was cleaning my hands?

"Help me back to the bed." I reached out, fumbling in the dark, until I felt the solid mass of his chest. My palms slid over hard muscle layered under smooth skin. I'd pushed and punched men's chests before while fighting, and I'd curiously examined the stable boy's physique. But I'd never fondled someone like this. I'd never let my hands flow over the contours of the abs, the pectorals—I'd never felt a tight nipple roll between my fingers. And I couldn't stop—my palms slid higher, along the bold lines of his collarbones, over the muscle-packed curves of his shoulders.

"What are you doing, Princess?" he whispered.

"I'm—I'm finding distraction from the pain," I murmured. "And I may be a little bit drunk. Is this—all right?"

"It's very all right." A light shudder passed over him. "It's been a long time since anyone touched me like this."

Like *this*—like what? How was I touching him? Like I was fascinated? Like I wanted him? Like maybe I didn't dislike him as much as I had at first?

I let one hand drift down his breastbone and explored his abdominal muscles. When they tightened under my touch, I sucked in a quick little breath of delight. I caressed the edges of the scars, circled the indentation of his navel, pushed my fingers along the ridge of muscle above his hipbone. My other hand stayed on his bicep, where I could feel tension thrumming along his arm, which hung stiffly at his side.

My skin sang and thrummed in response, and my lower belly, my hips, my thighs, everything inside me ached, with a power that almost superseded the occasional stabs of pain across my back. I remembered how the stable boy had stuffed his hands under my shirt, kneading and squeezing almost painfully. I suspected the Fiend Prince might touch me differently, and I quivered with the desire to know.

"You can—touch me a little, too." I barely breathed the impossible, imprudent words.

"Devil take me," he groaned softly, and his warm fingers slipped along my sides, moving upward until—oh yes—they smoothed over my breasts, and I sighed into the touch. The Fiend Prince didn't squeeze; he caressed, gently hefted the weight of each breast in his palms, teased the nipples with his thumbs. I could not breathe. I braced myself against his chest with both hands.

"Why does that feel so good?" I breathed.

"Because you need it," he said hoarsely. "You need it as much as I do."

"Need it?" I whispered. "Need what?"

"Pleasure, connection. Human touch that doesn't hurt, that has no agenda—you don't have an agenda right now, do you, Princess?" He kept fondling me, sliding one palm down my stomach, and I thought I might melt or explode from the colliding sensations of pain and pleasure. "This isn't some plan to elicit secrets from me?"

"No, no," I panted, while his fingers trailed along my hipbone. The space between my legs was hot, so hot—quivering, throbbing, wanting—

Touch me—

Panic blared through my body, panic at being so vulnerable here, in the Fiend Prince's bedroom, in the Cursed Palace of Terelaus. "You're—you're not looking, are you?" I gasped, and without thinking, I lifted my hand to where his eyes should be, to check if they were closed.

My fingers touched something gooey—a sucking gelatinous surface where there should be skin, a nose, a forehead—

The Fiend Prince cried out in pain, and I screamed too, staggering backward and shrieking again as my back twisted with the movement.

My eyes flew open.

21

The Fiend Prince's handsome face was gone. In its place was a slick mess of exposed viscera and raw flesh. And where his forehead should have been gaped a black, gelatinous wound, with ragged edges of broken bone as if something had blasted through his skull. In the center of the wound I could see wriggling pink brain tissue, moist and pulsing. His eyes bulged in hollow sockets, concealed by rotting lids, and his once-beautiful lips were ragged and bleeding. His whole face, the wounds and the remnants of his skin—all of it was spiderwebbed with glowing red lines, thin as strands of hair.

I screamed, short and sharp, and I gripped the washstand, dragging a towel from a shelf to cover my front.

The Prince's rotting lids rolled up, showing his dark eyes. "I knew it," he snapped. "This was a stupid idea."

He spun away and strode into the bedroom, shielding his wrecked face from me. "It grows back, you know." He kept talking, his harsh tones reaching me as I stood paralyzed in the bathroom, struggling to make sense of everything. "My face will be back to normal tomorrow morning. My body, however, will lose its strength and beauty within the hour. I'll be my weak, unappealing self again—probably even more feeble and scrawny this time. Too bad for you, Princess. You can have either the beautiful body or the lovely lips, but not both." His laugh was drenched in hideous bitterness.

I staggered back into the bedroom, fighting my pain and my horror, gripping furniture with one hand for support while I held the towel in front of me with the other.

The Fiend Prince's mask was back in place, a cold sneer that matched his tone this time. "So now you know the nightmare you've married. I'm either a brawny golem with a magic-rotted head, or I'm a desiccated skeleton with a pretty face. If you'd met me a year ago, I would have had both the physique and the magic to charm you. But now—well. It's useless, because you appreciate a good body, and I can't fault you for that."

"I'm not as shallow as you think," I managed.

"Of course you're not," he said dryly. "You didn't touch my body until it looked like this. That tells me all I need to know."

Pain seared my back, even as guilt seared my soul. The haze of the wine and the exhaustion was growing worse, and I wavered, clinging to a chair, on the edge of collapsing.

"Please," I whispered. "Please help me."

As I pitched forward he caught me in his arms.

He settled me face-down on the bed again, and drew the sheet up to my waist. As I sank into unconsciousness, I heard his broken whisper. "Why did you have to touch me?"

*****

I woke to a strange prickling sensation across my back, and the feeling of weight pressing me down. My fighting instincts kicked in, and I bucked, snarling at whoever was on me.

"You were right, Your Highness—she's a fighter," said an unfamiliar voice. "Good idea to have the guard hold her down. Peace, Princess—I am trying to heal you."

I stilled at once, submitting to what I now realized was a guard's hands on my shoulders, and the prickling of magic across my torn flesh. I turned my head to see the other side of the bed, where the Fiend Prince reclined against pillows. He had shrunk back to his lean, underfed aspect—bony protruding collarbones, sharp jaw, pretty mouth, and dark eyes that looked sad, so sad. He wore a loose white shirt with a ruffled collar, its drawstring neck unlaced, exposing the bones of his chest.

Looking at him, knowing what I knew, I felt a pang of impending loss. He was dying. His father was killing him slowly. And when he died, what would become of me? Nothing good, I'd wager, especially if there was no baby in my belly to ensure the Dreadlord's favor.

Beyond that, I would miss him, this ruined Prince. My existence had become inextricably wound with his, and I—I liked him. I liked his laugh, and his mind, and his tenderness. I didn't like his subservience to his father, or his resignation to this cycle that brought him closer and closer to inevitable death. I didn't like his lack of ambition or drive for his people and his nation's future. But those things could change, with time and with help.

Maybe my father could help us, if I could only get word to him. Maybe other nations who feared Terelaus and its Dreadlord could band together and defeat him if they knew what truly lay inside the Terelonian borders. The Terelonian shell, as the Prince had said, was a thin one, and the right application of pressure could crack it, eliminate the Dreadlord's dominance, and free us all.

The key would be killing the Dreadlord, or uncovering the secret magical substance his soldiers used. Or both.

And this Prince could help me with that, if I could persuade him.

Strangely, I didn't only want this for my own sake anymore. I wanted it for his.

He was pretending to read a book, but he finally cut his eyes over to me as I lay under the ministrations of the healer. "Do you want something, wife?" he asked.

"Many things, husband," I answered. "First, your name."

The healer clucked his tongue. "You haven't told her your name yet? For shame, Your Highness. He doesn't like his name, you see."

"My name is fine," the Prince growled.

"Then tell me what it is," I said. "You owe me that much, after—"

After I was forced to marry you.
After your father had me whipped.
After last night.

He cleared his throat. "It's Galanrae."

"Galanrae?" I repeated, trying to control the twitching of my mouth.

"See?" He glared despairingly at the healer, gesturing to me. "See her face? It's a ridiculous name."

"So I could call you 'Gal.' Or 'Rae,'" I said.

"Don't forget 'Lannie,'" added the healer. I liked him already, and I hadn't seen his face yet. He seemed to lack the half-frightened, saccharine reverence that most of the servants and guards showed the Fiend Prince. "I used to call him 'Lannie' when we were young."

22

Galanrae. I rolled the Prince's name around in my mind and decided I liked it after all. I would still tease him about it, of course, but secretly, in some part of my soul that I did not like to indulge, I thought it sounded romantic.

"That's it then, Your Highness." The healer ran a hand over my back, and I felt no pain at the touch. "Your skin might be a little itchy and red for a while, but it won't scar. Nasty wounds, those."

A servant brought me a robe and I slipped it on quickly. "Thank you for fixing me," I said, turning to face the healer. He had frizzy brown hair in knots all over his head, and each knot was bedecked with enameled pins. He wore thick, fur-trimmed robes, colorfully embroidered with pastoral scenes—deer, rabbits, trees, cottages. His skin was ochre, and he wore gold shimmery paint over his eyelids and pale pink color on his lips. His lashes sparkled with flecks of gold. "I am Onwe," he said. "A pleasure to serve you, Princess."

"Onwe is native to a land on the northern border of Terelaus," the Fiend Prince said. "My father occupied and conquered it when I was quite young. Even back then, as a boy, Onwe was a gifted healer, and very intelligent, so my father brought him here to be a companion for me."

"I later fell out of favor with the Dreadlord," Onwe added. "By the Prince's mercy I was not imprisoned or executed, but banished from the Cursed Palace and the surrounding towns."

"How are you here then?" I asked. "Will you be in trouble for coming to the palace?"

"The Prince sent someone to bring me here by secret ways," Onwe said. "We had to avoid a few new patrols, which is why I was delayed getting to you. And now I must go, before word of my presence reaches the Dreadlord. But first—" He rose and circled the bed, laying a palm to the forehead of the Fiend Prince. Their eyes met, and I saw a sorrowful doom in the healer's expression. "You are doing as well as can be expected," Onwe said, with forced cheerfulness. "Have you been able to—perform—as required?"

"Do you mean on the battlefield or in bed?" The Prince's mouth arched in a sneer.

"Both."

The guard who had held me down and the servant who had brought me the robe were both gone, and the three of us were alone. Still, the Prince's voice was little more than a whisper as he said, "The Princess and I have not yet consummated."

"What?" Onwe's eyebrows shot up. "But word throughout the Cursed Palace—and throughout the entire kingdom—is that the two of you are coupling like rabbits, so frenzied with passion you can barely keep your hands off each other."

"A well-acted ruse we have concocted together," said the Prince. He did not look at me.

"Well, I must congratulate you on playing your parts convincingly thus far, but I must also warn you that the king will not let you alone without proof for long. He will have her tested—" Onwe pointed to me— "to see if she is with child. And when the sorcerer tests her, he will know if she has your essence in her body or not."

I felt the blood draining from my face. "What are you saying? That a sorcerer would have some magical way to tell if I've been—intimate with the Prince?"

"That's exactly what I'm saying." Onwe nodded gravely. "Magic is closely linked with the focal points of the body's energy. The sacral locus resides low in the belly, and it is activated by intercourse. In women, when the—ah, the *essence* of a male is present, the energy of the area becomes blended, and that blending can be discerned and interpreted by a talented sorcerer like Andreas."

Andreas—the king's chief sorcerer, the one who bound my body with his green lines of magic, who scorched my tongue when I wanted to protest my marriage to the Fiend Prince.

"That's a very disturbing and invasive notion," I said haughtily, drawing the robe more tightly around myself. "How long is this 'blended energy' discernible after the—after the coupling?"

"For a week or two," said Onwe. He puckered his broad lips, regarding me and the Prince with serious brown eyes. "I know this makes things awkward, but I thought it fair to warn you."

"You excel at making things awkward, Onwe," sighed the Prince. "But we thank you for the warning." He rose unsteadily and embraced the healer, who muttered something in his ear and clapped his thin shoulder firmly. With a nod to me, Onwe glided from the room.

"Thank you!" I called after him again, and he lifted a hand in response.

I knotted the belt of the robe and paced around the room, rolling my shoulders and testing the freshly healed skin and muscle of my back. Everything seemed to be whole and functional. Experimentally I punched one of the chair cushions and was rewarded with a spray of feathers.

"You seem even stronger than before," said the Fiend Prince.

"You sound as though you disapprove."

"Not at all," he yawned. "But I am heartily jealous."

I turned toward the bed. Though I was looking at his normal face, austere and handsome, I couldn't help picturing the seeping, rotting wound of a countenance that had shocked me last night.

"You're remembering what you saw," he said. "Horrible, wasn't it? I knew it would affect your view of me."

"Not really." I shook my head. "Perhaps I pity you more now."

"Pity?" He scoffed. "*Pity*. How delightful. Exactly the emotion a husband wants to evoke in his new wife." He rolled over in the bed, burying his head under a pillow.

I stalked to his bedside and jerked the pillow away. "We need to talk about this," I said. "Do you think what Onwe said is true? Will a sorcerer be testing me? Will they be able to tell that we haven't been together?"

He kept his face pressed to the sheets, his black hair tumbling in a wavy mess over his ears. "It's possible," he muttered. "I've heard of court nobles having their wives magically tested when they suspected infidelity—that sort of thing."

"So there's truth in it. Damn." I sank onto the edge of the bed. "If the sorcerer tests me, and he finds out we've been lying, what will the Dreadlord do?"

23

The Prince didn't answer my question at once.

"Galanrae." I gripped his shoulder. "What will your father do when he finds out you haven't bedded me?"

"Nothing good." He flipped over, staring up at me with eyes that shone like dark stars in his thin face. "He might have you imprisoned, punished, removed from your station as my wife—that last is unlikely, though. To my people, the bond of marriage is untouchably sacred. It is meant to last a lifetime, and separations are rare among Terelonian couples."

"Then if not separation, what else might the Dreadlord do?"

The Prince turned his head away, and I saw a faint flush on his cheek. "My father might decide to supervise our consummation personally. To force it."

This was what I'd feared, but hearing it said aloud was a shock to my very soul.

I'd heard of kingdoms where royal wedding nights were supervised by nobles and courtiers, where ambassadors and high-ranking officials bore witness to the coupling of the pair. But those were the shocking customs of faraway kingdoms. Brintzia had never followed such traditions, nor did most of the nations around us. After all, some royal pairs in neighboring countries consisted of two women or two men, and creating an heir wasn't considered so all-important. In this part of the world, we were more enlightened, more civilized—or so I had thought.

Apparently Terelaus was the exception.

I could imagine the horror of being forced, of having my last few choices stripped away. It wasn't something I'd ever expected to face, being raised under my father's protection in the safety of the palace. Every time I'd grown anxious about my future husband, I'd reminded myself of my father's promise to me—that he would let me choose. That I could marry for love.

Never again would I trust in a man's promise to protect me. Because of my father's broken vow, I was trapped here, running out of options.

"I won't do it," said the Prince fiercely. "I won't do that to you. They can't make me."

"They could probably find a way to get your seed inside me," I said. "Magically or otherwise."

"Then I'll help you escape," he said. "I'll get you out of here, somehow. There's the passage Onwe used to get in—maybe I could smuggle you out that way. I could bribe someone to help—"

My heart jumped with hope, but I had to be realistic. "Everyone here is more afraid of your father than they are of you. They might not mind guiding a healer into the Cursed Palace, but I doubt you could find people loyal enough to help the Crown Princess escape. And if I did manage to get out of the palace, your father would send soldiers after me. Even if I made it home, my father would only pack me up and send me back here again, unless I had something to offer him, some sure way of defeating the Terelonian forces. He won't risk more Brintzian lives in defiance of the Dreadlord."

"Then you should go elsewhere, to another kingdom," said the Prince. "Maybe a country far to the south. You can take on another name, another identity. You can be free."

I hadn't seen such fierce eagerness from him since I came to the Cursed Palace, and a trickle of sweet affection raced through my heart. "What about you?" I asked. "Would you come with me?"

His mouth fell open, and he stared into my eyes.

I blushed, averting my gaze. "You deserve to be free, too. And I don't think I could be happy if I left you here alone to die, while I ran away."

"I can't leave," he said softly. "I have to stay with my people."

"But you're doing them no good here anyway," I countered. "You follow your father's every order, whether or not it's good for you, or for the kingdom. Maybe it's time you stopped doing that."

"Ah. So I should just stop obeying him, and let him kill me. Let him send me to my grave early, because I'm headed there anyway."

"That's not what I'm saying. I'm saying if you care about the Terelonians, as you claim to, maybe it's time to start acting on that. Maybe—" I lowered my voice to a whisper— "maybe it's time for someone *else* to go to his grave early."

His dark lashes blinked as understanding seeped into his eyes. "So now you want me to kill my own father."

"Maybe?" I grimaced.

"It's not that I haven't thought about it. After what he did to you, I actually made three different plans to kill him—if we could somehow eliminate the sorcerers who test his food and drink, check his rooms, examine his clothes, and scrutinize anyone who approaches him."

After what he did to you, I made plans to kill him…

There was something wickedly sweet in the Prince's speech, a dark, murderous romance in his tone that heated my core. But I couldn't let myself be distracted by that traitorous heat. We needed a practical plan.

"So magic is the thing that's protecting the Dreadlord. What if we took that away?" I leaned in eagerly, my body bent over the Prince's prone form. "How did you lose your magic? Maybe we could do the same thing to the king's sorcerers, and—"

But the Prince was shaking his head. "I don't know if the thing that took my magic still exists."

"The thing?"

He pressed a pale, long-fingered hand over his eyes, sighing. "It's no use, Princess. Any of these plans would take time, and that's something we don't have if they're planning to test you soon."

My nose prickled, tears threatening to gather and spill as desperation pinched my heart. "You won't even try. You talk a lot, but when it comes to action, you're pitiful. You're weak. And I'm not referring to your body."

I wrenched my face away to hide the oncoming tears, furious at myself for shattering so quickly. The Prince *had* offered to help me escape—though we both knew that wouldn't work in the long run. I desperately wanted him to be open to other ideas, ideas that included his own freedom, not just mine. I couldn't, I couldn't let him rot away here, alone—

The tears overflowed, and I let a soft sob escape.

Sheets rustled as the Prince sat up. He slid his hand across my back. "Don't cry, Princess. You're right, I've been as weak of will as I am of body. I've had no ally or confidante since Onwe was banished years ago. But now I have *you*. And you're twice as bold and dangerous as he ever was—stronger than I could ever be, in here." He touched my breastbone lightly, with his fingertips. "For you, I'll try. Do you hear?" He wrapped both arms around me as I crumpled against him. "You hear me, Princess? We'll try, together. And I know where we can begin."

24

The Fiend Prince sent away the guards and servants outside the door, giving them various errands that sounded plausible enough. Of course his real intention was to clear the way, so we could leave alone, just the two of us, and head for whatever secret parts of the Palace he wanted to show me.

When the hallway was finally empty, he took my hand and we dashed out of the room together. We had dressed in plain black clothing, and I'd bundled my hair into a loose knot.

As I hurried along behind him, my fingers interwoven with his, I realized that I felt strangely excited, and—and *happy*. It seemed sacrilegious, wrong in every way, to be happy here, in the palace of my enemies, in the company of the killer of my people, the man I'd been forced to marry. The man whose children I was supposed to bear so the Dreadlord could use them as pawns in his war.

"Does your father have magic?" I whispered.

"No. Mine was passed to me by my mother."

"And what happened to her?"

"She died of a sickness she contracted while lending aid to plague victims," he said. "I was not allowed to see her during the weeks she was ill. My father wouldn't risk my health."

"Yet he risks it now."

"Yes, because he is careful of me only when it suits his goals." The Prince motioned for me to wait while he peered around a corner. Another moment, and he waved me on. "Some men are cruel to the world, yet manage to love their blood-kin. But my father feels nothing for anyone. He is fascinated by human emotion, intrigued by it, because he cannot sense it and does not understand it. I've seen him question criminals and prisoners of war about their emotions during long torture sessions. He loves to toy with the feelings of others, like a clockmaker might tweak the cogs of his timepiece."

"So does he use the substance that you use, the one that gives power?"

"No." The Prince emitted a brusque laugh. "He needs to stay hale and hearty so he can dominate everyone. The toll it takes isn't something he wants to inflict on himself."

"Then why wear a mask?"

"Perhaps he believes it makes him more fearsome, more inhuman, more *dread*ful."

His sardonic tone made me snicker in response, though I winced internally at how callously the Dreadlord inflicted on his son what he would not endure himself.

"We are out of the area where the sorcerers usually prowl," said the Fiend Prince. "We may walk a bit more freely for a while." He ushered me into a broad corridor and we strolled down it, past stiff armored guards in glossy black helmets. None of them stopped us, though they shifted uncomfortably as we passed, probably wondering why we had no guards escorting us.

More hallways, and a few sets of a half dozen steps up and then down, and down again. Finally we halted before a gigantic set of ebony doors inlaid with scarlet stones that swirled as if flames were trapped deep inside them.

"This is the library," the Prince whispered to me. "We have to cut through it to get where we're going."

I nodded, my heartbeat kicking into a faster rhythm.

The Fiend Prince gestured to the men flanking the entrance, and they pushed the doors wide for us.

"You have no personal guards with you, Your Highness," said one of them.

"I wanted none," the Fiend Prince replied haughtily.

"But is that wise, with—" The guard's helmet tilted toward me.

The Fiend Prince moved with the speed of a striking snake, gripping the man's bare neck right under the edge of his helmet. "Are you questioning me?"

In his voice I heard the echo of his father's harsh tones, and I suppressed a shudder.

"No, Your Highness," faltered the guard.

"Good." The Prince released him and caught my wrist, drawing me through the doors.

The library was as gloomy and dire as the rest of the Cursed Palace, outfitted with ornate bookshelves of carved black hardwood, stocked with dark leather-bound tomes. The Prince tugged me along, burying us deep among the rows of books; and then he let me go and set his back to the shelves, bending over and breathing hard.

"You should be resting," I told him. "You're still recovering from whatever you took, the stuff you won't tell me about."

"I endured the worst of the recovery last night while you slept," he said through shaking breaths. "But yes, I have perhaps overdone it this morning. I had to put a lot of strength into that choke-hold to make it convincing. They cannot know how weak I am, or they will respect me even less."

"How do you know that?" I asked. "Maybe your guards and servants would love you, rather than fear you, if they knew what you've gone through. And I'll wager they know a lot more about your current state than you think. The servants in my father's palace know everything. They always find out the secrets we try to conceal from them."

"A skill you seem to have absorbed from them," he said wryly.

I shrugged, smirking. "Everyone has something to teach. I'm not so foolish as to ignore the practical wisdom of working men and women just because I have a title."

"Smart woman." He looked up at me and smiled, and my heart exploded with the warmth of his approval.

I clenched my hands, trying to tell myself I didn't care what he thought. "Can you go on?"

"A moment." He breathed deeply. "Why don't you take a book or two while we're here?"

"I'm not much of a reader," I admitted. "I prefer real live adventures to those on a page. I don't like to sit around staring at words.

"I never used to read much either. I was always traveling, fighting, training, attending galas, entertaining lovers." His smile went crooked, and my stomach thrilled. "I do a bit more reading now, though." He pushed himself away from the shelves. "Let's go."

The library was like a maze within a maze—a labyrinth of intersecting aisles, so dimly lit it was a wonder anyone could find what they wanted in there. The Prince led me to a back corner stuffed with fur-cushioned chairs and draped with heavy blood-red curtains. An enormous painting of the Dreadlord hung on the wall between the drapes.

The Prince pushed aside a bit of one tasseled curtain and slid back a panel on the wall. "Keep watch," he whispered.

"Um—all right…" I scanned the nearby aisles. They were too shadowed for me to see far. "No one's coming."

He was spinning some mechanism within the wall, pressing toggles and clicking levers. Finally, with a deep clunk, the wall swung inward.

"Classic secret passage," I said casually, as if I wasn't frightened or impressed. "We have a few of those at home."

"I doubt they lead anywhere as unpleasant as this," he said. "This is a back door to my father's research area, where his sorcerers perform magical experiments. The main entrance is much too heavily guarded for us to access, but he and I have the code to this door."

"Secret magical research?" I peered into the blackness beyond the opening. "And this will help us figure out our problems?"

"It's a start. We have to be very quiet, and we cannot be caught, do you understand?"

"I'm not usually the spy type," I said hesitantly. "I'm more of the brawling type, the hit-first-and-ask-questions-later type."

"You underestimate yourself, darling," he said. "You've been sly enough during your time here. You can do this."

He was already halfway into the black corridor, his body bathed in veils of darkness, his pale features sharper than ever and his eyes glittering. He stretched out one bone-white hand to me. "Are you coming?"

25

I eased into the dark hallway with the Fiend Prince. When he closed the secret door behind us, it whirred and clicked. Locked again.

There I stood, buried to the eyeballs in inky black, unable to see anything. Panic fluttered in my gut as I remembered what had happened the last time I couldn't see the Prince. How he'd fondled me, and how I'd touched him, and the terrible end to that interlude.

Suddenly all I could envision was his magic-rotted face. The corridor felt too stuffy, too narrow.

"Princess." His voice seemed muffled by the closeness of the space. "Your breathing is very quick. Are you all right?"

"I can't see. It's too tight, too narrow. Can we go somewhere else, please?"

His fingers fumbled across my waist. "Where's your hand?"

I intercepted his hand with mine, and he gripped it, warm and reassuring.

"Come with me." He wrapped my arm close to his body, and we moved along the hallway. After a few minutes I saw a soft glow ahead.

"What are we looking for, exactly?" I whispered.

"We're here to see if the thing that took my magic is still here."

"What thing?"

"You'll see. I can't explain it very well—it's something you have to witness for yourself."

We came to the end of our passage, which intersected with a longer, better-lit one. The new hallway was broken up by doors, some of them open and some barred by locks and chains.

The Fiend Prince pointed into a few of the rooms, whispering their purpose to me. "See those glowing bottles on the shelves? Those are energy and essence samples. Very hard to capture and purify. There's the distillery where they collect and process the essence. And that's where they store odd items created by magic, things that aren't useful for war, but are interesting examples of magical ability."

He sidled up to a corner and checked for guards before motioning me to proceed. We crossed the space quickly, and I glimpsed several soldiers standing in the right-hand hallway, conversing together.

When we were out of earshot of them, he said, "That heavily-guarded hallway has several vaults for magical weapons, and for devices used to focus magic. We take those items into battle with us sometimes. And down here—" he pointed ahead—

"are the magical artifacts we haven't figured out yet. The thing that took my magic is the worst and most powerful of them all."

"What about the substance you take to restore your powers?" I asked. "Where is *that* made?"

"Same hallway as the vaults, just farther down," he replied. "There's an intake area for the raw materials, and equipment for extracting and processing the substance."

"And you still won't tell me what that mysterious substance is."

He eyed me sidelong. "Soon."

"Is it what your father's hunting for? The reason he keeps conquering more nations, expanding his territories? He's looking for more of it?"

The Prince's eyes lit up with that keen look of approval again. "You're quick, Princess."

"But Brintzia doesn't have any magic, or magical substances," I protest, ignoring the compliment. "We get one or two sorcerers a generation, maybe, but nothing like you're talking about. Nothing that gives powers to normal humans."

"You think you don't have it," said the Prince. "But you don't realize the treasure you possess."

Frustration galvanized my limbs and drove me into action almost before I thought. In half a second I had the Prince's thin body pinned against the wall, my hands laced around his throat. "Do you like keeping me in suspense?" I hissed. "Is it fun for you, watching me scramble after the slightest clue and struggle for scraps of hope?"

"Maybe a little fun," he wheezed through my grip.

Enraged, I tightened my fingers, and he choked. "Fine, it's not!" he gasped. "It's not fun at all! I realize what's at stake for you. And I'm trying to trust you, I really am. But think of my position, Princess. If I trust you completely, I could lose everything. You will pass the information to your father somehow, and he will act on it. When Terelaus falls, what do you think will happen to me? Do you think the nations my father has subdued, the people he has conquered, will be forgiving? Do you think they'll let me go on living in peace?"

He gagged, and I loosened my grip a little. "I don't suppose they will."

"No. I'll be killed for war crimes, or imprisoned for the rest of my life. So in revealing my people's secrets to you, I am ensuring my own doom."

"Your doom is ensured anyway. At least this way you have the chance to do what's morally right."

"Such a comfort."

"You could run," I told him. "Go south, as you told me to do, and live in some faraway land."

"You'd let me side-step the consequences of a lifetime of bloodletting?"

"I—I suppose. I did ask you to run away with me," I growled.

"You did, didn't you?" He smiled wonderingly at me. "I think I undervalued the significance of that moment."

"It was a moment of madness, clearly. I have no idea what possessed me to say that, because I *hate* you. I hate you, and your father, and this horrible place."

He stared at me, his dark eyes liquid, his pulse fluttering under my palm. And I hated him more because he felt so helpless in my hands, because he didn't fight back, because his long frail form simply relaxed against the wall, yielded to my will.

"I deserve all your hate," he said quietly. "Hate me with all the strength and passion of that beautiful fierce heart of yours. Crush me and break me if you must, in retribution for everything I have done, all the bodies I've broken, the blood I've spilled. Break my neck, Amarylla. End it, if that will bring you peace. You've wanted to kill me since that first night—so do it. Just a twitch of your fingers. Go on."

He tipped his head back, and like a fool I noticed the crisp angles of his jawline, the tender skin under his chin. I noticed the thick sweep of his dark lashes, and the soft prettiness of his mouth.

"I want to kill you," I whispered. "But I can't."

"Because I'm your way out of this."

"Maybe."

"Or because you like me."

"I just said I hated you."

"My mistake." His mouth curved in a smile, soft with sadness despite his teasing words. "If you'll let me live a bit longer, I can show you the thing that took my magic. And perhaps then some of your questions will be answered."

26

My anger ebbed, and I dropped my hands from the Fiend Prince's throat. He stepped away from the wall, massaging his neck.

"Thank you for sparing me," he said quietly.

"Just get on with it," I mumbled. "Show me this thing you keep talking about."

"It's right this way—if it's still here."

He led me along a short corridor, which ended in a thick-plated iron door. No one was on guard there, perhaps because nothing and no one could ever enter such a well-defended entrance. I could not even count the number of locks and bars and bolts securing it, in addition to magical sigils that glowed faintly red. The door seemed impossibly huge, so big that three or four horses could have charged through it abreast.

"It's in here?" I ran my finger along one of the bars.

"It was." The Prince unlatched a few smaller bars and swung aside a great metal shutter, revealing a thick pane of polished quartz, nearly transparent. "Look through, Princess, and witness the instrument of my doom."

Through the clear slab of stone I glimpsed a room dimly lit by the Cursed Palace's ubiquitous amber crystals. In the center of the chamber swayed a hulking shape—leathery wrinkled skin, mountainous shoulders, and a blunted head with six tiny eyes that swiveled wildly back and forth. The creature was big as a cottage, with great sagging jowls that dripped saliva onto the stone floor. Where the saliva struck, it sizzled and smoked. The walls of the room had been scored over and over by the beast's claws—claws that gleamed poisonous green in the gloom.

"What is that?" I breathed.

The Prince leaned in next to me, the waves of his black hair tickling my cheek. The licorice-and-pepper scent of him spiked in my nostrils, a heady wicked fragrance that made me want to kiss his mouth, to see if it tasted as deliciously spicy as he smelled. I blinked away those thoughts and focused hard on this revelation, this *thing* that had somehow taken his magic.

He spoke in a low, regretful tone, tinged with awe. "That is a monster of the ancient world, unearthed and dragged here as an inanimate carcass—then revived by the darkest and most powerful spells ever wrought in Terelaus—or anywhere else in the world."

"Powerful magic? Like the magic wielded by Andreas, your father's chief sorcerer? Did Andreas bring an ancient monster to life?"

"Andreas, yes, and other sorcerers in my father's employ. And it cost the life-blood of two dozen Terelonians. I was there when the sorcerers performed those human sacrifices and woke the beast. I tried to stop them from slaughtering our own people to feed that creature's vitality, but I failed. And when the monster broke out of its bonds and attacked us all, I was one of the victims."

I gasped with understanding. "That's where your scars came from."

"Yes. The monster tore into me with poisoned claws, and its toxin neutralized my powers. My superior strength disappeared, along with my other abilities. My father demanded that his sorcerers heal me, but many had been damaged in the attack and had lost their own innate abilities. The ones who were left could not knit my ravaged flesh together—it was contaminated by the poison, and my body resisted their magic. I barely survived, and I was left with a visible mark of that night."

Shock and disbelief colored my tone. "Why would your father want to restore life to a long-dead monster?"

"Because of its—" But the Prince broke off suddenly as voices echoed along the hallway, the one adjoining our bit of corridor.

"Someone is coming," he whispered, his eyes frantic. "We're not supposed to be here." He closed the metal door over the window and replaced the latches.

"Is there another passage?" My own whisper was tremulous. "A way out?"

"No. But perhaps—" He fumbled with the handles of nearby doors. One gave way, and he pushed me through it, following me in and shutting the door quietly.

The small space we'd squeezed into was as stuffy as the secret passage from the library had been. I chafed and squirmed against the shelves sticking into my back.

"Be still." The Prince's words were barely audible, a breath against my forehead. He was jammed right against me, and I thanked the stars he wasn't in his bulkier muscled form, or we would never have both fit into the closet.

The voices grew louder. Probably a patrol coming to check on the monster's cell.

"All quiet, as usual," said a female voice. "Let's move on."

"We need to check the bolts and locks," replied a male voice. "And we're supposed to test the magic seals, too. You know the drill."

"It takes so long," groaned the woman. "No need to do it every round."

"I won't be the one blamed for a security breach," replied the man stoically. "We check it all."

I bit back a groan. I would have to spend an indefinite number of minutes pinned against the Fiend Prince, barely able to breath the musty air. I couldn't stand tiny spaces like this. Being confined with no way to move freely, no route of escape or room to fight—I couldn't stand it. I couldn't be still. Sweat broke out on my forehead and under my arms. If we didn't get out soon, I was going to burst.

Desperate, I reached for the Prince's hands and gripped them spastically, trying to communicate my panic to him. He shifted closer, and his profile skimmed against mine in the dark, nuzzling gently, a soothing brush of skin. He hadn't shaved, and his jaw was lightly stubbled. As his rough cheek grazed my smooth one, I felt a delicate tingle deep inside me.

I went perfectly still.

The Prince's lips skimmed my cheek, his soft breath warming the hollow of my ear. Mutely, instinctively, I yearned toward him, the tips of our noses bumping lightly, nudging. My lips parted, accepting his light exhale. I tingled all over, a buzzing ache rolling through me, my hips pressing to his.

27

Through the cloth of his trousers and mine, I felt the Fiend Prince harden, firm and wanting. Wanting *me*, the wife he'd been forced to take. A normal physical reaction to the proximity and the friction. It meant nothing, of course. He'd have the same reaction to anyone else if he was smushed into a closet with them.

The voices continued in the hallway outside, and though my pulse was still racing, my grip on the Prince's hands eased. But when his lips bumped lightly against mine, I clutched him again, an involuntary reaction. He hesitated, his soft mouth floating against the thin, sensitive skin of my lips.

"That's done, then," said the man. "On we go."

Booted feet clumped away, down the corridor.

"Amarylla," whispered the Prince.

At the gentle utterance of my name, a violent pulse of delight raced through my body, but I only gasped, "I need air."

He opened the door, and I practically fell into the hallway.

"We need to get back to the library before anyone else comes." The Prince's cheeks were red, and he wouldn't look at me. He checked around the corner, then whispered, "I can still see them. Wait… wait… and now."

He ducked out into the hallway, and I followed. We hurried back the way we had come, quickly, quickly… and then the staccato tramp of more booted feet spurred us ahead and we ran, swiftly and quietly.

"Just up here," panted the Prince, pointing to a dark doorway ahead.

But the guards' feet and voices were close—too close. They were about to round the corner. They would see us before we reached the safety of the library passage—

I ran faster, gripping his wrist and yanking him along with me. We ducked into the passage a scant half-second before the sound of the oncoming feet clarified and the voices grew louder. They were in the hall, approaching quickly.

"Do they patrol this passage too?" I whispered.

"Yes, and they carry lights. They'll see us even if we run."

"What will we do?" I tried to summon my usual defiance, my will to fight—but fighting these guards would not do us any good. I would only end up being punished, or worse. "I don't want to be whipped again." The words burst out of me, a quiet, desperate plea.

The Fiend Prince's shadowy form advanced on me in the dark. His hands closed on my arms, and he pushed me against the wall and kissed me just as a pair of guards stepped into our passage, lifting a light to inspect the space.

I barely had time to register the shocked expressions on the guards' faces before my eyes fluttered shut, sealed themselves blissfully because my body was humming with a delirious compulsion, focused on the place where the Prince's lips molded to mine.

He tasted fiery, dark, and sweet. That spicy heat of his mouth—it was as addictive as I'd imagined. I craved it, relished it, swept my tongue between his lips seeking more of it. He smacked one hand onto the wall above my head, a delighted murmur rolling through his chest as he shifted closer. My hands traveled to his backside, pressing his hardness to my aching core. His wet, silky tongue slid over mine, and suddenly I needed more of him against me, in me. I let the longing ripple through my throat, a hum of desire.

"Your—um, Your Highnesses." A guard's tentative voice sifted through the hazy lust in my mind. "You can't be back here."

The Fiend Prince broke our kiss, peering over his shoulder at the guards. "Oh, hello! I'm so sorry—I'm afraid we got carried away. We were in the library, you see, and we just wanted a little more privacy, so I thought we could just step into this passage. I suppose it was a foolish idea."

"No one but you and the Dreadlord are supposed to use that door," said the guard firmly.

"Of course, of course. A momentary lapse. I blame it on my wedded bliss." The prince grinned. "I'm the luckiest man, truly. But we'll go. So sorry for the indiscretion, and thank you for your diligence."

The guards didn't stop us as we moved along the passage, back toward the secret door leading into the library. I could hear them muttering anxiously behind us. But what were they to do? If we'd been deeper into forbidden territory, they wouldn't have believed the Prince's explanation, and they would have detained us, questioned us—perhaps punished or imprisoned me. But they'd caught us so close to the library—and the Prince's act had been so very convincing—

I didn't dare hope we'd gotten away with it, not until we'd passed through the gloomy channels of the library and made it back to the more familiar areas of the Cursed Palace. When we reached the Fiend Prince's suite, his guards were back at their stations. Their helmets hid most of their faces, but their mouths were grim, a sure sign that they knew they'd been tricked into leaving so we could wander without an escort.

"Sire," said one of them, the stout woman I'd sparred with the other day. "You and the Crown Princess should not be wandering the palace alone."

"But we weren't alone," he said cheerfully. "We were together. I was showing her the library." He added the last phrase in a sultry, significant tone, and the guard shifted her stance awkwardly.

"Very good, Your Highness," she said. "Next time you would like to show the Princess around the palace, we will be happy to escort you. It is our duty, and failing in our duties would bring the wrath of the Dreadlord down upon us *all*." She emphasized "all" in a heavy tone that sent cold fear into my stomach. This was a warning, that they would suffer if we broke the rules again. That *I* would suffer.

"Understood," said the Prince quietly. His hand touched the small of my back as we entered the bedroom together.

28

Two servants were in the Prince's suite, tidying up and arranging the random items he had sent them to fetch. One of them had brought a tray of prettily iced buns and steaming mugs of cider. The Prince and I took chairs in the seating area, and I sipped gratefully from a mug. The hot liquid soothed my nerves.

Neither the Fiend Prince nor I spoke until the servants stopped bustling around us and finally heeded his hints for them to leave.

"They're worried," I told him, when the bedroom door had closed. "They could be punished for letting us slip away, couldn't they?"

"It's possible. The guards would be more likely to get in trouble." The Prince leaned back, taking a large bite from a bun. A bit of the icing smeared on his lower lip, and when his tongue swept out to clean it, I watched, transfixed, remember how that tongue felt in my mouth.

He chewed slowly, watching me.

"The guards who caught us in the passage—will they tell the Dreadlord?" I asked.

"They might. And he won't be so quick to believe that we were simply carried away with passion." The Prince took another bite.

"Which means he may decide to check up on us," I said. "On *me*."

"I won't let him hurt you again." The Prince leaned forward, his dark eyes burning. He looked so intense and earnest, yet so pathetically thin and fragile. I could hardly bear it, and I repeated the words back to him internally, a silent vow.

I won't let him hurt you again.

"We were interrupted before," I said. "I'd like to pick up where we left off."

A sensuous awareness brightened his eyes. "Would you now? I might be tempted to go along with that."

"Oh, I didn't mean—" I flustered. "You were going to explain to me why your father dug up a prehistoric beast and sacrificed his own people to bring it to life."

"Oh, that." He shifted in his chair and cleared his throat.

"Unless you've decided not to tell me after all," I said. "You don't trust me completely, and I understand. It's difficult to trust anyone when your own blood has betrayed you." I thought of my father's betrayal, when he gave me up to Terelaus. Objectively I understood that my life wasn't worth the lives of thousands of people—yet I still wished my father had made a different choice, or found some other way. My father had been far kinder to me that the Dreadlord had been to his son, but still,

I could understand a little of the Prince's caution and apprehension.

"You threatened to kill me again, very recently," the Fiend Prince pointed out. "That isn't traditionally conducive to trust-building."

"I only threatened you because you wouldn't tell me the things I want to know, things that could help us both escape all this," I said in a low, sharp tone. "I didn't actually kill you, did I? So there. In fact, I'd go so far as to say I consider you an ally."

"An ally?" He regarded me with a dark, analytical expression.

"A—a friend."

"A friend?" His voice dropped lower still.

"Yes, a friend," I murmured, my face warming again. "What more do you want to be?"

"No more than I already am." He crossed his long thin legs and cocked his head aside. "I will tell you about the monster and its purpose. But you must promise to answer three questions honestly when I am done. Any three questions I choose, and you reply with perfect honesty. Agreed?"

"How do you know I won't lie to you?"

"Because you, Amarylla, are an honorable soul. Yet another quality a king might prize in his queen."

I buttoned up my lips and pondered the ways in which he might twist this bargain to his advantage. "I won't share state secrets about Brintzia."

"Your people surrendered already. Neither my father nor I have any need of Brintzia's secrets. We own them all."

My eyes flashed up to meet his. "And do you own me?"

"No."

"Good answer." I pulled my legs up into the chair and crossed them, setting my elbows on my knees. "Very well, Galanrae—we have a deal."

He winced at the use of his real name.

"You really do hate it, don't you, Galanrae?" I let my voice slither over the syllables.

"A little less when you speak it," he said.

He had that look again, that vulnerable, hopeful look that cut right down to the quivering core of my heart and turned me into a puddle of empathy. It was all I could do not to leap from my chair and hug him tight and kiss him all over his pathetic, pretty face—

He smiled at me, his lashes blinking slow over his dark eyes, and my breath hitched.

"The deal is struck," I said brusquely. "On with your explanation, Fiend."

"Very well." He leaned back in the chair and began. "Long ago, before man emerged as a dominant species, this world was populated by great beasts who possessed intrinsic, natural magic. Their power was raw and unfocused, but tremendously strong."

"Where did they get their power?"

"No one knows. And even what I'm telling you now is only a theory put forward by the Dreadlord's sorcerers. When my father and Andreas were young men, roaming the North and wreaking havoc in the name of their own glory, they discovered the preserved carcass of one such prehistoric beast. A member of their band cracked open a bone of the petrified monster and found strange iridescent ichor inside, still liquid after thousands of years. My father fed a bit of the ichor to a slave, and the woman gained a temporary burst of strength and magic."

I gasped, gears whirring frantically in my mind. "You're consuming ichor from some old preserved beast's bones?"

"Technically, yes. My father killed most of the people with him on that excursion, so he could preserve the secret of the ichor until he was ready to use it. Once he and Andreas had figured out how to refine and employ the substance, he began giving it to Terelonian soldiers under the guise of a magical tonic. To this day, most Terelonians do not know the true origins of the tonic they're given. They drink it at my father's command, and they battle for Terelaus until the side effects become too severe, and their bodies wear out. And then the Dreadlord calls up more soldiers, and poisons them all over again."

"It's horrific," I said. "And it sounds unsustainable."

"My father doesn't give the tonic to everyone," the Prince said. "He has been strategic with it, until recently. But yes, no matter how carefully he doles it out, no matter how skillfully he spends the lives of his people, it is an unsustainable system."

"And what is he planning to do once he runs out of people?"

"He has already begun conscripting soldiers from conquered lands," said the Prince. "It is a never-ending cycle of greed, you see. He wants more ichor, so he conquers more lands so he can search beneath their soil for petrified monsters. But to keep his hold on the new lands, he needs more enhanced soldiers, which necessitates still *more* ichor, which means he must expand his holdings yet again—and on it goes."

29

This was beyond what I'd imagined. Ichor from an ancient beast, giving magical strength and abilities to otherwise normal Terelonians. No wonder the armies of Terelaus were so powerful, and so greatly feared. But the side effects of the substance, the gradual draining and decay of its users—that was a terrible price to pay for an empire.

"If Terelaus doesn't collapse first, your father will continue consuming men and women, won't he?" I asked. "He will keep finding more soldiers and feeding them ichor, so he can conquer new lands and find *more* ichor."

"Exactly." The Prince nodded. "Brintzia should keep him occupied awhile, though. Your people have quarries and bogs where such monsters are likely to be preserved intact. My father believes your entire kingdom to be rich with ichor. He'll send in teams to pull out the beasts' bodies, and sorcerers to conceal the secret work from the people of the land. It's what he does in every nation he conquers. Then he'll take your father's armies as his own."

My father's armies. My people would be conscripted, dosed with ichor, and sent off to fight the Dreadlord's wars until they met the same fate as the Terelonians.

So my father's surrender and his gift of me to the Dreadlord's son hadn't saved our people at all. Everyone in Brintzia was still doomed to die—except instead of dying in battle, they'd be dying slowly from the toxic ichor in their bodies.

"Don't your people realize what's being done to them?" I asked. "Don't they understand that their ruler is killing them? They should be able to see the correlation between their use of the tonic and the acute suffering when it wears off. Why don't they simply refuse to drink it?"

"My father has convinced most of them that Terelaus suffers from a widespread plague that leads to weakness and early death," the Prince said. "Terelonians believe that the strength and abilities they enjoy after drinking ichor is their true state, as they were meant to be. The sorcerers tell everyone that drinking ichor staves off the plague, so the people clamor for it. They believe they will die much sooner without it. Most of them can take it for several years before they finally succumb to its effects."

"How long have you been taking it?"

"Only a year." He examined his own thin fingers, the joints sharply pronounced, the veins showing blue-green through his pale skin. "The decline has been extremely rapid for me, probably because I once had true innate magic. Andreas isn't sure how the monster's poison interacted with my body's chemistry to negate my powers. And he has not been able to reverse the damage."

"Then we're back to my original question—why would your father revive such a beast?"

"He didn't know about the poison," the Prince said. "He craves power, and he thought if the petrified bones of a dead beast yielded such valuable essence, the body of a live one might do even more. When you think about it, it's hilarious how thoroughly his plan backfired. He wanted to increase my power, as the greatest of his warriors—but he ended up losing me instead."

"You're not lost yet," I said firmly. "And lucky for us, the monster with the magic-removing poison is still alive. So now all we have to do is collect some of that poison, dose your father's sorcerers with it, and then—" I stopped short, but the Prince knew what I was about to say. To achieve any freedom for Terelaus and the subjugated lands around it, we would have to kill his father—or imprison him, at the very least.

"You should talk of treason in a quieter and less jubilant tone," the Fiend Prince said dryly. "And now that I've answered your innumerable questions, it is your turn to answer three of mine."

He rose from his chair, circled the low table between us, and with a soft rustle of black velvet he perched on the arm of my chair. His licorice-and-pepper fragrance sifted into my nose, muddling my head.

I drew away and glared up at him. "What are you doing?"

"I felt too far away from you. This way I can look right into your eyes when you answer, and I can discern the truth of what you say."

"I thought you trusted me to tell the truth."

"To a point, yes. You'll tell as much truth as you're able to with your words, and the rest you'll tell me with your eyes... and with your body." His light voice circled me, snared me, weaving a wordless spell.

I would rather have faced an opponent on the training mats than bare my mind to the Fiend Prince of Terelaus. But I wasn't one to yield to fear. I lifted my chin, holding his gaze. "Ask your first question."

"What do you think of me?"

My stomach flipped and my jaw dropped a little, but I managed to keep my composure. "I think you are well-meaning, intelligent, and humorous. I don't think you are willfully cruel or murderous, but you've let yourself be led, when you should have been bolder in defense of what's right. However, I recognize that if you'd rebelled against your father, you might be dead now—so I can't fault you too harshly for that. You have admirable qualities, but your fear and your physical frailty are like veins in the rock, weakening it. Your physical limitations don't have to hold you back, though. You can still do the right thing—defend your people and claim your kingdom. You can make repayment for some of the blood you've spilled. I will help you do it."

"All right, all right." He pressed my shoulder lightly, but I felt his touch like a brand. "Your answer turned into a motivational speech."

"You wanted the truth." I rose out of the chair, partly because I felt so strongly about what I was saying, and partly because I didn't like looking *up* at him. "You're better than this. You're better than a blade in your father's hand. You don't have to end any more innocent lives."

We were nearly at eye level as he perched on the chair arm. I'd laid my hand on his knee during my impassioned speech, and I had leaned in—close, too close. Emotion quaked in the air between us.

"You really want to help me," he said. A statement, not a question.

"I do," I said. "You're not the monster I thought you were. You're human—strong and fragile—" My eyes flicked to his perfectly shaped lips, slightly parted as he listened. "You're a killer, and I keep trying to remind myself of what you do on the battlefield, because when you're here, you show me a side of you that's so different…" My words trailed away, dissipated in the scintillating tension between his mouth and mine.

"Second question," he breathed. "Honest answer."

"Hmm," I murmured.

"Do you want to kiss me?"

30

Did I want to kiss him?

Honest answer... no lies...

"The kiss in the library passage was just for show," I said.

"That's not an answer, Princess."

"*You* kissed *me*. I didn't—I don't think—"

"Amarylla." His lips curved in a smile as warm as the glowing fireplace behind him. In that moment, the world was sweet-hot cider and black velvet and quivering flame. "Do you want to kiss me?"

My heart took over, a swift yearning impulse propelling me forward. My fingers clasped his thin face, and I took possession of his perfect mouth, claimed it tenderly with my own lips. He responded with an eager hum in his throat.

There must be a cord tying the mouth to the sacral locus of the body, because with every sensuous slide of the Prince's lips against mine, that cord carried waves of tingling pleasure all the way down to nestle and throb between my legs.

The Fiend Prince rose from his perch on the chair and wrapped an arm around me. His other hand worked its way deep into my hair, cupping my nape, while he sucked and tasted my mouth as if I held the sweetest honey on my lips and tongue.

We kept kissing, tasting, breathing into each other, until our lips were swollen and flushed. A thrumming heat glowed between my thighs, a sweet ache that yearned for him, for hardness and wholeness inside the soft slick places of my body.

"I want something," I whispered.

"Anything," he said hoarsely.

"I can't stop thinking about how you touched me the other night." The night when he came to me with that glorious, magically enhanced body, and we explored each other. I could barely believe I was asking, but, "Would you ever want to touch me like that again?"

"Gods' bones, yes." The words were a desperate moan. The Prince scrabbled at the buttons on my shirt, but his fingers trembled. With a swift jerk, I popped the buttons and tore my shirt off, letting it fall. I wore nothing underneath, and his eyes widened, glazing slightly at the view of my uncovered breasts.

"Your turn." I seized his collar and tore his shirt open, too, baring his lean scarred torso.

"There's not much to see here." He grimaced as he pulled his arms out of the shirt and discarded it.

"I like it." I gave him a smile, half shy, half daring. "Because it's you."

A tender pain shone in his eyes as he approached me again, his palms gliding along my waist—but a noise at the door startled us both.

"Damned servants," he hissed. "Come here, quick."

He grabbed my hand and we raced into his closet, burying ourselves in the lines of hanging clothes. There was a space at the back where I'd hidden myself once before, and he sat down on the plush carpet, pulling me into his lap, between his legs.

The murmur of servants' voices reached us, and the clink of the tray and cups being gathered; but they left without coming to look for us. Perhaps they guessed that we were hiding, engaged in something salacious. Though this time, it wasn't an act. I was really half nude, leaning back against the Prince's bare chest.

In the dark, his slim fingers crept over the soft warm flesh of my breasts, smoothing and fondling them. His delight in their size and form showed in the repeated twitch of the hardness pressed to my rear.

Rigid I lay, scarcely breathing, exposed and exhilarated and a little terrified. While he caressed me, I wrestled inside, torn and enflamed. I didn't *want* to want him, because his father and mine had arranged this. I didn't want to crave his body, to lust for his touch. But he was starting to slide one hand down, along my stomach, past my navel and across the quivering flesh below it.

"Last question, Princess," he whispered, his breath hot and intimate against my ear. "Do you want me to make you come?"

"You mean—" I breathed, barely able to think.

"Do you want me to give you that burst of pleasure you haven't been able to experience yet?"

"Bold of you to think you can," I gasped, as his fingers teased beneath the waist of my pants.

"Give me a chance." He kissed my earlobe and cupped his other hand more firmly over my breast. "And give me an honest answer."

His wandering hand settled between my legs, over the trousers, and my spine arched involuntarily, my hips bucking into the pressure. "Yes," I whispered. "Yes, you can try."

"Thank you," he breathed, as if I was the one doing him a favor. "Take off your pants for me."

I unfastened them and slipped them off along with the undershorts I wore, and then I resumed my spot between his legs. The plush thick carpet felt naughtily delightful against my bare backside.

The Fiend Prince's lips brushed my temple as he spoke. "First I'm going to titillate you, to see what you like."

I gripped his thighs in the darkness, my legs pinned tightly together, waiting.

The tip of his finger stroked me, right along the crease between my legs, and I mewed. I couldn't help it.

"You're very sensitive, sweet wife," he whispered. "I don't think this will be too difficult. Spread your legs for me, just a little. That's right. Open for me."

His gentle male voice in my ear was doing half the work. I'd never been touched or spoken to this way. The stable boy had been laconic, monosyllabic, and rough. This was velvet and wine and whispers, a delicate seduction.

"This bit, right here at the top, is key to the pleasure," he said, fondling a small nub at the apex of my folds. "I can do this—" he circled it slowly with a wet finger— "or this—" he pinched it gently and rubbed it with two fingers, and I trembled, gripping his legs tighter. "Ah, the second one stimulates you more. You see, it's all about learning what your body wants and needs. And now we're going to explore a bit lower. You're so silky and soft, Princess." His fingers plowed gently through my folds, one finger dipping a little deeper than the rest, testing the slit at my center.

"You don't have to do this," I panted. "It's—it's messy, and you—you'll be bored—"

"Do I seem as if I'm bored?"

"N-no…"

"I have the beautiful warrior Princess of Brintzia helpless and panting in my arms, and I get to teach her how to enjoy her body. This is the best thing I've done in years—maybe ever."

Piqued at him calling me *helpless*, I writhed angrily against him, and his breathing went ragged. "Amarylla, don't move like that or I won't be able to focus."

"Don't tease me," I said shakily. "It's hard for me to let myself be here, with you—to let you do this—don't make it more difficult, please."

"I'm sorry." He kissed my temple, my cheek, the corner of my jaw. "Let me make it up to you."

31

The Fiend Prince spread his whole hand over my core and began to move it rhythmically, circling, pressing. The stimulation was exquisite, dizzying, unbearable—I inhaled sharply, almost a breathy shriek, as his finger dipped inside me—one at first, and then two. Then he toyed with the sensitive nub again, jiggled and massaged it until I was gasping, loud and desperate. Two fingers glided into me again, deeper this time, thrusting faster and faster while he shifted his other hand over my breast, teasing my nipple erect.

I had never felt so much sensation at once. Frantic for release, I struggled and writhed, my body damp with sweat. But I couldn't make the sensations *break*, or crest, or whatever they were supposed to do, no matter how hard I concentrated.

"You're fighting it, Amarylla," said the Fiend Prince, his lips soft against my ear. "Stop fighting it. You can relax. You're with me—you won't be hurt. Let yourself go."

"I—I can't." My voice shook, tears welling in my eyes. "I'm trying—I don't know what I'm supposed to do—I'm sorry—and you're working so hard—but I can't—"

He stopped thrusting into me with his hand and leaned around, pulling my face to his. "You aren't supposed to do anything. There is no obligation here. Would I love to be the one to make you come for the first time? Yes! But it's all right if you don't. This is practice. We are learning your body, together."

He kissed me—a deep, heartfelt, sealing sort of kiss, and I felt the tension easing from my muscles and bones. My limbs went slack, and I laid one hand along his neck as I kissed him. Slowly he began to massage my folds again, kissing me until I broke the contact between our mouths and arched backward, whimpering. This time I didn't fight. I let myself trust him, and I let the sensations inch slowly upward toward whatever peak awaited.

The Prince tended me cleverly, listening to the sounds I made, adjusting his motions to suit my pleasure, building layer upon quivering layer until finally something crystallized and shattered, pulsing in shimmering circles through my belly. Half-sobbing with relief, I arched into his hand and he bent over me, nursing me through the waves of bliss and murmuring, "Yes, yes, darling. Yes."

Entirely limp, I lay across his legs, naked and damp and dizzy with pleasure. The faintest glow from the bedroom sifted between the hanging clothes and laced across my body. By the same dim light I saw the Fiend Prince's beautiful thin face, and his dark eyes devouring the sight of me.

"Do you mind," he said jaggedly, "if I please myself a little, too?"

Gratitude and affection pulsed warm in my heart. I would not remain in the Fiend Prince's debt, oh no.

I sat up and scooted closer to him. "What if I say no? What if I forbid you to pleasure yourself?"

"Cruel girl," he whispered. "But I would obey."

"Then obey me in this," I said. "Remove your clothes, and let me touch you as you touched me."

He sucked in a quick breath. "If you like."

"You may have to guide me," I warned him. "The stable boy I was with simply hiked up my skirts and pulled down my pantelettes and pushed himself inside. I didn't have much time to explore him."

"You've told me so little about this stable boy, yet I hate him so much," said the Prince cheerfully, rising to shuck off his pants. "I suppose he was muscular? Beautifully shaped? No scars?"

"Yes to all those things," I replied, getting to my feet. "But you—" I sidled closer to him as he stood, now naked, with that generous length bared to my view— "you are far more beautiful." I pressed a palm lightly to his chest. "You—" I kissed him— "are a magnificent fiend." Another kiss, and my fingers closed around the warm silky length of him, sliding upward, shifting down, tugging softly.

He groaned, deep and helpless. "More of that," he said hoarsely. "Smoother and faster. Rub your thumb over the tip. Ah—"

I sank into the rhythm, stroking quickly and firmly along the shaft, up and down. He made those familiar sounds, the sounds he'd faked before to fool the servants. I caught some of them with my mouth, savage searing kisses against his open lips.

"I'm not going to let you die," I whispered to him, nuzzling his sharp jawline. He was bowed over, clutching me, his thin body tight and hard with anticipation. "You belong to me now."

At those words he jerked and spasmed in my hand, his release jetting onto the clothes, onto me. I threw both arms around him, pressed our bodies together while he panted against my shoulder and rode out the last bit of the pleasure.

"The servants will have to do extra laundry," I said, smothering a giggle. "Does it always do that when you come? The—fountain?"

He chuckled. "Yes, that's how it works. Of course in the case of couples trying to reproduce, the 'fountain' would happen—inside—"

"Inside me," I whispered. I'd known how it worked—the general idea of it anyway—but this was intimate, immediate, and visceral in a way that I hadn't expected. "I barely felt it when the stable boy did *that*, in me. I suppose I'm lucky I didn't get pregnant."

"If you had, maybe you wouldn't have been forced to marry me." The Prince pulled down the garment he'd soiled, folded it over, and used it to clean first himself, then me. "Your life might have been better in that case."

"Easier," I said. "But maybe not better."

Something shy and fragile floated in the dark space between us.

"I should have asked you already," he said. "Was there someone else back home, someone you wanted to marry?"

"No. You?"

"There were a few women I watched, but none who stirred my heart like you do."

My heart shuddered and throbbed hot as he moved in, gliding long fingers down my arms.

His tone was quiet, edged with passionate sincerity. "If I had my choice of all the princesses, all the nobles, and all the working women of the world, I would still select you as my bride. I could not imagine being married to anyone else. I wouldn't *want* anyone else. Just you—you brutal, beautiful, brilliant woman."

32

His confession took me by surprise. My mouth went dry, and words fled my mind entirely. I couldn't think how to respond—what to say—and then the seconds ticked by and it was too late, too awkward—

The Fiend Prince dropped his hands from my arms and stepped back, nodding, his lips stiffening. "It's all right," he said. "We can be allies who occasionally pleasure each other. No need to reciprocate my feelings."

He threw a dressing gown around himself and stalked out of the closet. After donning a similar garment, I followed him, twisting my hands together, trying to conjure up some humor to lighten the moment. Every joke I thought of sounded too silly, even hurtful, considering what he'd just expressed—that if he'd been given the choice, he would have chosen me. Over every other woman in the world.

How could anyone handle an affection so strong? No one had ever cared about me like that, ever.

"We'll need to go to dinner soon," the Prince said, jabbing viciously at the fireplace logs. "My father doesn't expect us to dine with him daily, but tonight he will."

I swallowed hard, the awkwardness fading beneath my rising anxiety. "I haven't seen him since he had me whipped."

"Nor have I. He'll be gauging our reactions carefully. We must act penitent, and subservient, even as we—" The Prince looked at me significantly, and I nodded, understanding what he didn't voice. *Even as we plot against him.*

I moved to his side, speaking in a low tone. "Is there anyone you can trust in the Cursed Palace? Anyone who might be loyal to you over your father?"

He chewed his lip, his profile starkly amber and gray in the firelight. "I can think of a handful. My cousin Kallaran hates playing the officious toadie to my father, but he makes himself useful so my father won't consider him a threat to the throne and have him killed. And there are a few men and women I've fought with who might bear me allegiance."

"What about the servants who tend you here? And your personal guards? If you explained your situation to them, might they help us?"

"It's a big risk. Any of them could decide to report me to my father."

"Can you bribe them? Most people can be bought."

"I have little wealth of my own. It's all my father's, and I must request what I want. But I do have some things of value."

"Knowledge will likely be our greatest weapon," I mused. "You said that most Terelonians believe the ichor to be the solution to a nationwide plague, yes? What if we told them the truth?"

"Rumors of the truth have circulated before," the Prince said. "My father has always managed to squash them and make them seem ridiculous."

"But if the truth came from you, it would have more weight," I countered. "And what if you had the support of another monarch behind you? My father, for instance? The night he sent me to you, he whispered in my ear, asked me to discover the source of Terelonian magic. If we could get a message to him—"

The Fiend Prince turned, his dark eyes ominously bright. "He wanted you to spy on me? What am I saying—of course he did."

"Yes, but I—"

"And you have done a marvelous job playing the spy." The Prince made me an elaborate obeisance. "And I played the consummate fool. The Dreadlord warned me against letting you worm your way into my heart. Women, he said, are deceitful tricksters. Emotion is the enemy. And I ignored his cautions, idiot that I am. You extracted everything from me." He laughed bitterly. "You paid me well, in there." He jerked his head toward the closet. "But you used me, didn't you? Those things you said, about wanting to help me—was any of it true? Or was it all part of a masterful spy's game?"

"I haven't lied to you."

He scoffed and turned away. Desperate for him to understand, I caught his thin wrist and jerked him back to face me. "Everything I said was true," I hissed fiercely. "I'm your friend, your ally. We're in this together. We share a common cause, and I refuse to let you waste away under your father's hand, or in a prison cell. I will find a way to get you clear of this, because your soul is worth saving. You deserve a path to redemption."

"What about the monster on the battlefield?" The anger faded from his eyes, leaving them sorrowful. "The one with the sword that drinks souls, the one with the whips of fire? The one who has slaughtered countless soldiers from many lands? Is *he* worth saving?"

"Yes," I answered stoutly.

"Why?"

"Because your wrongdoing comes from weakness, not willfulness. And weakness can be bolstered and corrected. Weakness can be exercised and helped. You're not malevolent and apathetic, like the Dreadlord. You can change. The information I wanted from you was for my own benefit, yes—but it's for yours too! If we apply the right pressure at the right points, we can do this. We can take down your father."

The caution in the Prince's eyes made my heart ache. I'd wounded him when I failed to reciprocate his feelings. And he was trying not to care, but for someone like him, someone who'd had so few to love him—I could only imagine how painful the apparent rejection must have been.

But it wasn't a rejection, not really. It was my own stupid brain, tripping over something I never thought possible—that my forced match with the Fiend Prince could turn into something real, and sweet, and powerful.

I could try to tell him how I really felt—but I still didn't have the right words, and he wouldn't believe me if I spoke now. All I could do was wait, and show him, through every action of mine, that I cherished the gift of his heart, and that his trust in me had not been misplaced.

"Come," I said, swiveling my fingers from his wrist to his hand. "Let's call the servants and dress for dinner. We've got a Dreadlord to fool and an insurrection to plan."

33

Dinner with the Dreadlord was a sweaty-palmed, tight-fisted affair. I had to bite my tongue a few dozen times to keep from lashing out with some mocking words or rebellious comments. The Dreadlord had the audacity to ask how I was feeling, with a smirk that was clearly discernible beneath his half-mask, and I gave him a prim, polite answer.

We skirted the topic of my punishment, and he did not mention how the Prince and I had been caught in the secret library passage. Maybe the guards hadn't told on us. Maybe they were afraid that if they mentioned it, they would get into trouble somehow. The entire Cursed Palace seemed to exist in a constant state of fear.

As we walked back to the Prince's suite after dinner, trailed by a couple of bodyguards, I whispered, "So all these guards and servants take the ichor?"

"Most of them," he whispered back. "But rarely. They are led to believe that the 'cure' is in short supply and must be rationed. The soldiers are given more frequent doses. But look." He pointed to a guard standing at the intersection of a passage. Her muscles swelled and her fingers sparked purple as she fingered the hilt of her sword. "She's had a dose recently. Probably because she's guarding the hallway leading to the treasury. She'll enjoy the effects for a few days before they wear off, and then she'll crash."

"I don't understand why these people don't grasp what's really happening. It seems obvious."

"People can be brainwashed to believe almost anything," the Prince said. "And some of my father's sorcerers have a persuasive influence that softens the mind, makes it more susceptible to unquestioning belief."

"All the more reason to take the sorcerers out." I spoke a little louder than I meant to, and he squeezed my arm with an anxious glance behind us.

"Hush, Princess," he said quietly.

I glanced back too. One of the guards following us was Betta, the strong, stocky woman I'd sparred with, the one who'd requested a healer for me after my whipping. Her presence, and the memory of her kindness, triggered an idea.

When we arrived at the Prince's chambers, I said, "Betta, I'd like to speak with you."

"Me, Your Highness?"

"Yes. Come in here for a moment, will you?"

The Fiend Prince frowned at me, as if wondering what I was up to, but he didn't protest, and when he and Betta and I stepped into the room, he went to the bathing area and left us alone.

I closed the bedroom door and pulled her close to the fireplace. "Betta, you seem compassionate as well as strong. Do you guard the Prince often?"

"It's one of my primary duties, Your Highness."

"Wonderful. So you're loyal to him?"

"Of course."

"Take off the helmet, please, Betta. I'd like to see your face, unobstructed."

Betta obeyed, her forehead seamed with concern. "I'm flattered, Your Highness, but I have a husband—"

"Gods, no." I laughed. "I'm not looking for another bedmate. What I'm proposing is far more dangerous."

Her eyes narrowed. "Go on."

"What if you knew that someone was threatening the Prince's health, his wellbeing, his very life? How far would you go to defend him?"

She squared her shoulders, her mouth grim. "I would remove the threat."

"Very good." I moistened my dry lips and went in for the kill. "And what if the person threatening him were important, and highly placed?" I stared intently into Betta's eyes. "What would you do then?"

Awareness flared in her gaze. "If that person were threatening the well-being of my beloved Terelaus as well as the Prince's life, I would be even more motivated to remove the threat. But I could not do it alone."

"None of us can," I agreed. "Which is why you and I are having this little chat."

She nodded. "There are others who would lay down their lives for Terelaus and the *Prince*." She emphasized his name, an unspoken exclusion of the Dreadlord. "More than you would think. The people are desperate, and confused." She glanced quickly at the bedroom door. "I must return to my post, but I will send someone to you who can speak further of this."

"Good. Thank you."

Betta was halfway to the door when she turned back. "How do I know you are not simply trying to uncover and root out the rebellious flowers?"

I cast aside my caution and let a steely edge creep into my tone. "I value my freedom," I said. "I do not appreciate being banned from training, and whipped, and treated as a womb for the incubation of the Dreadlord's next set of weapons."

"Fair enough." Betta nodded, satisfied. "And the Prince?"

I gave her a small smile. "The Prince will do as I say."

A flicker of admiration and humor passed through her eyes right before she jammed her helmet back on. "It was a happy day when you came to us." And she left the room, closing the door quietly behind her.

When I turned around, the Fiend Prince was leaning in the doorway to the bathing area. He looked so pale, graceful, almost skeletal—the fragile beauty of him snatched my breath. His eyes were narrowed to dark slits. "I'll do as you say?"

"Won't you?" I said lightly, brushing past him.

"What did you tell her?" He followed me into the bathing room and watched me adjust the spigot for the tub. I hadn't bathed in a few days, and as the steam rose from the hissing water, I felt immensely grateful for the plumbing in the Cursed Palace.

"You can call the servants to help you with bathing, you know," said the Prince.

"No need. I didn't often ask for their help at home, and I'm happy to handle it myself here as well. As for what I said to Betta—don't worry, I was very careful. She's loyal to you, not your father, and there are others who feel the same way. She promised to put them in contact with me."

"You work fast." Admiration tinged his voice.

"That's the best way to work."

"How do you have so much energy always?"

"I just like getting things done." I tested the water with two fingers and looked up at him. "Are you going to let me bathe?"

But before he could answer, two servants appeared in the doorway behind him. "We're here to help you prepare for bed, Your Highnesses."

"I think I'll bathe," said the Fiend Prince, his eyes fixed on mine. He spread his arms. "Disrobe me, please."

34

My jaw dropped. I wanted to swear at him, to call him a few of the foul names I'd spewed right before our wedding ceremony. But the servants were supposed to think we were happily married.

"*I* was going to bathe, dear," I said sweetly.

"Of course," he said. "There's just enough room for two, darling. It will be so cozy, don't you think?"

The servants already had his coat and waistcoat off, then the shirt, and the pants, and then he was entirely naked, sharp bones and lean flesh, and that sweet smirking mouth.

He was playing with me. Testing me.

Well, two could play at this game.

The servants moved to me, and I let them strip off my outer layers, my hoops, my corset and pantelettes—all the trappings of fine evening wear—until I stood as naked as him. There was a good deal more substance to me, though—smooth muscle and firm flesh, heavy breasts and strong thighs. My stomach, legs, and arms were toned from training. I reveled in my own strength as I stood bare before him, as I saw his eyes turn hungry, saw the twitch and stiffening of his lower parts.

He turned his back quickly, striding to the tub and seating himself in it. Thoughtful of him to spare the servants the sight of his arousal, though I supposed they were used to the exposure. In the Cursed Palace, as in my own kingdom, the royal personage was to be revered in all stages of dress or undress.

"Go," I told the attendants. "Freshen the bed, or something."

They looked to the Prince for permission, and he nodded. "But first, some herbs for the water."

One of the servants scattered dried herbs and flower petals over the surface, and they both moved out to the bedroom area.

I crossed my arms and glared at my husband. "You stole my bath."

He leaned back in the big claw-footed tub, his arms resting along its pale porcelain sides. "Your bath isn't being stolen, but shared. As I said, there's enough room for two. The tub may not be that long, but it's quite deep."

"Bastard."

He grinned, obviously aware that once I got in, my legs would have to interweave with his in order for us both to fit. "Come, wife. You may not love me, but you find me tolerably appealing, yes?"

My heart twinged with sweet pain, but I wasn't ready to yield yet. "I could simply pick you up and lift you right out of there."

"Come on then, warrior princess," he said, smiling wider. "Do it."

Because then of course his wet naked body would be pressed against mine. "Cocky ass," I hissed, climbing into the tub. I sat at the opposite end, with my feet practically in his crotch and his long legs stretching on either side of mine.

But my irritation faded for a second in the bliss of hot water sloshing over my skin. I yielded, sinking a little lower into the heat, closing my eyes and feeling tension drain from my muscles.

"This feels amazing," I murmured.

The Prince reached over and took a sponge and soap from a stand near the tub. "If you won't let the servants bathe you, will you let me do it?"

"Absolutely not. I can do it myself."

"I know, I know," he said, half-smiling. "You can do everything yourself. Except the one thing I did for you earlier."

A blush crawled into my cheeks. "I'll learn how to pleasure myself. Then I won't need you at all."

He sighed. "Yes, yes, you are the self-sufficient, independent princess. Strong and capable, doing what must be done, all by herself. Barreling through tasks like a runaway cart-horse."

"And you are the reliant, dependent prince, following the instructions he's given, and doing what he's told like a little bleating lamb headed for slaughter," I snapped.

His cheeks flushed bright red and his jaw hardened. The next second he flung the wet sponge at me. It hit my right shoulder with a loud splat.

I picked it up and threw it straight at his face. Water sprayed from the impact, and he spluttered and cursed. My glare melted into a giggle, and his face changed instantly, brightening as he lunged for me, sponge in hand. "Come here, Princess. Time for your bath."

I squealed and tried to scramble away. He caught me, drawing me toward him through the water and swiping my face with the sponge. The next few minutes were a tangle of slick gleaming skin and gasps and splutters, writhing limbs and breathless laughter and soap suds.

Somehow it ended with me in his lap, facing him, with my knees arched over his thighs. Barely breathing, I kept my eyes locked with his while he passed the soapy sponge over my breasts and along my sides.

He slathered soap over my belly and then slid the sponge down, between my legs. "I need to clean you thoroughly, Princess," he whispered. "You're very dirty, you know."

Whenever he said naughty things to me, I warmed from the inside out—and my reaction was even stronger with his arousal so prominent, so temptingly near. It wouldn't take much to put him inside me. I wanted to, with an aching compulsion that flushed my skin and throbbed at my core. But first I needed to prove something to him—that what I felt went beyond physical need or sensual curiosity.

"Give that to me," I demanded, wresting the sponge from his grip. With it I bathed him, from face to feet, lingering over his lower belly and his hips and his inner thighs. When I passed the sponge over his privates, he released a beautiful groan that sharpened to a whine as I stroked more firmly.

I stopped immediately, letting the sponge float away while I pulled my body flush with his, my ankles knotted behind his waist and my sensitive parts pressed right against the hard length of him. I laced my hands behind his neck, through his hair, and I kissed him, slow and tender.

"I'd choose you too," I said quietly.

35

The Fiend Prince leaned back a little, catching my gaze, a startled joy waking in his eyes.

I'd choose you too.

I nodded, affirming the words I'd spoken, my lip trembling. Why did I feel like crying? I turned my face aside, letting my wet hair cover the welling tears.

"I wish I had the ichor right now," he whispered. "I'd pick you up and carry you straight into the bedroom, very dramatically, and I'd put you on the bed, and I'd slip inside you and it would be exquisite, Amarylla. But it would also be what my father wants, and I won't do that unless you want it for your own happiness. Not for any other reason."

I tucked my mouth against his cheek and said softly, "But doing that would protect us, too, wouldn't it? Because if a sorcerer tests me, then our energy would be—blended. Which is what they want to see. We wouldn't be consummating for your father, not really—we'd be doing it for our own safety, and because—because I want to. If *you* want to."

"Oh, I want to." His voice thinned, raw with need.

"Then come on, Fiend." I forced a smile, a shield over the naked longing of my heart. I wanted him, but I didn't want to *cry* through this—warrior princesses didn't cry when they made love to their fiendish princely husbands.

But maybe they cried when the fiendish princely husband looked so heartbreakingly thin and pale. Maybe they cried when they could see Death slinking up behind him with a great scythe. Maybe then a warrior princess could cry, and rage, and catch Death by the wrists, and hold back that scythe with every ounce of will and strength she had.

The Fiend Prince was already slinging a towel around himself. He snatched one for me and offered me his hand, so I let him help me out of the tub. We dashed into the bedroom together and the Prince cried, "Out, out!" to the servants. While they scuttled into the corridor I plaited my hair into a quick braid and blotted the drenched, dripping end with the corner of my towel.

Then the towel was gone, torn free by the eager fingers of the Prince, and he collided with me, hard planes of ascetic flesh and bones. Our mouths crushed together and our bodies tangled, frantic and frenzied.

We crashed onto the bed. He was breathing so fast that concern spiked in my brain, cutting through the haze of lust. I drew away a little and put my hand on his chest. "Take a minute," I said. "Breathe. Calm yourself."

He nodded, sucking in deeper breaths, closing his eyes while his heartbeat skittered wild under my hand. After a moment, when his inhales were less shaky and shallow, I kissed him again, slowly, luxuriating in the hot, silky feel of his mouth, spiced with peppery darkness. We were amber honey and red wine, melancholic sweetness and sharp richness mingled.

His palms skimmed my body, and I put my hands on him gingerly at first, then more boldly, gauging his preferences by the hums of pleasure in his chest, by the jerk and throb of his length against my thigh. He liked my nails running over his shoulders, grazing his back. He liked my kisses along his collarbone, across his chest. He liked a teasing touch on his inner thigh, and a stroking finger along his spine, all the way down to his backside.

But it was hard to focus, hard to take note of what he wanted because all the while he was so skillfully manipulating me, eliciting delicate tingles and surges of pleasure, stimulating those nerve endings until I was squirming, nearly squealing. This time I knew exactly what kind of release lay ahead. I'd reached that pinnacle once, and now my body knew what to do. My stomach tightened, but other parts of me softened, turning liquid and ready.

"Lie back," I whispered to the Fiend Prince. "Let me do this part."

He stretched out, and I took a moment to delight in every inch of him. Not gloriously muscled, not a perfect male specimen—scarred and faded from what he once was, but I loved him in that moment, with a glowing intensity that threatened to explode through my skin and shine for all of the Cursed Palace to witness.

I arranged myself over him, fitted him into me, and he released a blissful moan. He was so much longer than the stable boy—so much more satisfying. Slowly I moved at first, experimentally, then faster—and the faster I rode him, the better it felt.

The Prince half-sat up, lips parted, eyes hooded with luscious want, and I leaned in to kiss him. That shift, the new angle of our bodies—it sent a thrill deep, deep through me and I said, "Oh," softly into his mouth. I'd never felt anything like that tantalizing friction, inside and out.

He clutched me while my thighs flexed, moving me up and down. Our voices chorused desperate, creating the symphony we'd tried to imitate on our wedding night—but nothing could ever be as lovely as the real thing. My voice went shrill, wild, and far beyond my control as my body spasmed around him, quivering and pulsing. A throaty groan exploded from him, synchronized with his hot release inside me.

And it was done.

Not to please the Dreadlord, but to please *us*. To protect us from his prying eyes and punishing orders.

The Prince and I slid apart, and when he turned on his side, slack and panting, I arranged myself at his back, with my body curved protectively around him.

"Are you all right?" I asked him.

"Better than all right," he answered. "Weary, though. I should sleep."

"I wish there was a way to get back your magic," I whispered against the crisp edge of his shoulder blade. "You could have your strength and your other abilities again, without resorting to ichor."

"If there was a way to restore me, Andreas would have found it, and my father would have told me about it," he said. "The Dreadlord wants nothing more than for his weakling son to return to his former strength and glory."

I chewed my lip. "Are you sure?"

"Of course. That's why he's making me drink the ichor, so I'll be strong again and I can fight for him." The Prince's voice was getting muzzy with sleep, so I didn't press the matter—but I wondered.

The Dreadlord wouldn't be the first ruler to feel threatened by his rightful heir. Galanrae was far into his twenties. If he were healthy, strong, and magically gifted, he'd be the ideal choice to take the throne—the great Seat of Ghast. In fact, a prince like that could have galvanized the entire country, rallied them behind him.

Maybe the Dreadlord didn't want to risk such a coup. Maybe he planned to use up his son's remaining strength and then let him die, hopefully after he'd fathered a grandchild or two. Then the Dreadlord could have many more years in power, with no threat to his position. He could brainwash and manipulate his vulnerable little grandchildren for years—and then, when he was old, one of them could take the throne and carry on the Dreadlord's legacy.

It's what I would have done had I been a malevolent, rapacious ruler completely lacking in all natural affection.

If the sorcerers *had* found a cure for Galanrae, would the Dreadlord have shared it with him, or kept it a secret?

36

My mind would not stop churning through everything I knew, all the facets of the ichor situation, and all the possible strategies the Dreadlord might have. I had to scoot away from the sleeping Fiend Prince, lest I wake him with my fretful movements.

Finally I flounced out of bed and padded across the floor to the door. I could have rung for a servant, but I didn't like to make a fuss, not in the middle of the night.

When I poked my head into the corridor, Betta pushed herself away from the wall and straightened. The other guard stiffened as well. "Your Highness?"

"Would you mind asking someone to get me some warm milk, or tea?" I asked.

"I'll find someone," Betta said quickly. She strode away, and I retreated into the Prince's suite.

Several minutes later a servant with brown hair and plain, unremarkable features entered the room, carrying a tray with tea and milk. "Your Highness," she whispered, with a glance at the sleeping Prince. "Betta said you requested this."

"Yes, thank you." I motioned to the low table by the fire.

The servant set down the tray, but she did not leave. "She also said you needed something else. A way to secure His Highness's future, and the good of Terelaus."

My eyes flashed up to hers. She gave me a small conspiratorial smile.

"You're the one Betta spoke of," I breathed.

"One of many who want change," she said. "They will move when I speak. I have been waiting for the right time, and it appears that time may be at hand. But first, tell me one thing, Princess—will your Prince be different from his father? Because Terelaus cannot take another Dreadlord."

"The Prince is weak of body, and in the past he's been weak of will," I told her. "But with support, I think he can be a good leader. One who listens, and does no harm to his people."

"Doing no harm is a good start," she said. "I'm told you have a plan?"

In whispers I explained all about the ichor, and the beast from the ancient world, and its poison.

The servant stared. "So the tonic we're given—it's not a cure for the plague of our people? It does not restore us to our natural state?"

"No." I winced sympathetically.

"I thought we were all born to be physically strong, and gifted with magic," she murmured, gripping the back of a chair. "Our priests tell us that Terelonians in their natural state are the most physically powerful and magically blessed beings in the world. We were made to rule all civilization. The lore says that our enemies in the surrounding kingdoms concocted a plague to weaken us, to make us normal like them, so we could not achieve our birthright."

"Your natural state is like everyone else—average strength, and no magic," I said gently. "The tonic—the ichor—it gives you powers, and steals away life and energy in return. Terelonians die young because of the Dreadlord's 'cure,' not because of some non-existent plague."

The servant wavered where she stood, and when I motioned for her to sit, she collapsed into a chair. "I thought the Dreadlord was withholding the cure, doling it out only briefly to those in his armies, those he favored. I thought it was a way of controlling us. I wanted revolution so we could make the cure freely available to all Terelonians."

"The Dreadlord has withheld things from you, just not in the way you thought," I said. "The people who take the tonic all have similar types of magic, right? They all wield it in the same way, in battle—nets and whips and pulses of energy. The people with unique magical abilities, like traveling magic or mental manipulations—they are born with a special gift, with innate magic. They are the natural-born sorcerers."

"So the Prince was a natural-born sorcerer," murmured the servant, glancing at the bed. "That would explain why his magic changed. He has always wielded whips and bolts of red fiery energy, but he used to have other abilities too—he could draw darkness around companies of soldiers, or form shadows to fool and distract the enemy. He could craft columns of whirling black cloud to tear through our enemies' ranks. But a year or two ago he stopped controlling the clouds and shadows—he restricted himself to wielding energy, like the rest of the soldiers."

"That must have been around the time when the beast attacked him," I said. "How do you know all this, about the way he used his magic on the battlefield? You're a servant—you haven't seen him in battle."

"My wife is a captain," said the servant. "She tells me what she witnesses on the field. Each time she returns home for a brief respite, she's a little weaker. It's the reason I began gathering allies, so we could overthrow the Dreadlord, get control of the cure, and save her. And everyone else, of course."

"To save anyone, we must end the Dreadlord's reign," I whispered. "And to do that, we must get past the sorcerers who guard him constantly."

The servant pondered, tapping her lips. "You said that the ancient beast's poison can eliminate a sorcerer's gifts?"

"Yes. We have to break into the research area, get through all the locks on that huge door, and drain some of the poison from the creature's talons. Then we have to give the poison to the Dreadlord's sorcerers." I leaned back in my chair, limp with discouragement. "Too many obstacles. I have no idea how we could ever get through that massive door to access the creature."

"You may not have to," said the servant. "I think I know where to get some of that poison."

37

"My wife is one of the Dreadlord's trusted captains, as I mentioned," said the servant. "And because of her rank and her trusted status, I was assigned to serve in the chambers of the Dreadlord. I never found the opportunity or courage to do him harm myself, but I watched everything. I noticed two items that he never removes from his person, except to bathe. One is a necklace with a tubular pendant—I thought it was a narrow bit of precious stone until I saw the liquid swirling inside. He keeps it tucked beneath his clothes. And there's a bracelet with an identical pendant."

"And how does that help us?" I asked, my fingers twisting with impatience.

"I'm getting to that," she said. "Once, while I was helping to dress him for a dinner with his chief sorcerers, I asked if he wanted to leave the necklace and bracelet off, and switch them out with something more glamorous. The Dreadlord said, 'No, on this night of all nights I should wear them. They are my safeguard against betrayal by those conniving magical serpents."

I gasped. "He keeps some of the poison with him, in case one of his sorcerers tries to turn on him! It makes sense that they would be his biggest threat—they are gifted with strong innate magic, and he has none."

She nodded eagerly. "I'll wager his closest personal guards carry some of the poison, too, and there may be more hidden elsewhere in his rooms. I no longer serve in the King's chambers, since I asked one too many questions—but the guards there still know me, and would probably let me in if I had a plausible errand. I'll try to find this poison."

"Be careful," I told her. "This could be a deadly mission."

"I know it." She smiled, and her dull face turned suddenly bright and beautiful. "For the people and the kingdom I love, I would risk anything."

She rose from the chair, giving me a curtsey. "A pleasure to speak with you, Princess. I'll contact you again as soon as I can. Until then, wait, and enjoy your new husband. And get some sleep."

After she left, my nerves and brain were electrified. Even with the tea and milk, sleep did not come to me for hours. I woke early and sat staring at the Fiend Prince, trying to *will* him awake, eager to tell him about what I had learned and the ally I'd made.

But he didn't stir.

Finally I leaned in close, intending to kiss him awake. The instant my lips touched his forehead, I knew something was wrong. His skin was hot as a kettle, and his breath was shallow.

I leaped for the cord and rang frantically for the servants.

For the next few hours I prowled the edges of the room, unable to get close to Galanrae as the servants and a court physik clustered by the bed. My heart brimmed with impotent anxiety. I'd never been good by a sickbed. I hated fevers, coughs, vomiting, all those things—things I couldn't fix, things I couldn't work on until they went away. So I let the servants and the physik bustle around my husband, while I shrank, too nervous to insert myself and demand a place at his side.

Halfway through the morning a servant stopped by, requesting that the Fiend Prince report to the Dreadlord in the war room at once.

"Can't you see what's going on?" I snapped. "The Fiend Prince is ill. He won't be coming."

The servant looked me up and down as if he didn't think much of me. Then he went away.

He'd been gone only a handful of minutes when the door to the Prince's suite exploded inward and the Dreadlord himself strode in, masked and cloaked, with heavy weapons and chains jangling at his belt. "What's this nonsense about the Fiend Prince being ill?" he thundered. "I need him on the front lines today."

Like cockroaches scuttling away before a harsh light, the servants and physik scattered from the Prince, clearing a path for the Dreadlord to see his son, pale and sweating. The Prince was murmuring to himself in the throes of a fever dream.

"Now you see," I said quietly. "As I told your messenger, he cannot come."

The Dreadlord's masked face swiveled sharply toward me. "Have you done something to him, you godsdamned cow?"

Blood roared into my face, but I responded as calmly as I could. "I've done nothing but bed him well, as you desired. This is something *else*, I think." I gave him a hard, intense stare, hoping he would discern what I could not boldly say. *His weakness is your fault, Dreadlord, not mine.*

After a moment's staring at me, the Dreadlord said, "Why have you not summoned a healer?"

"The servants told me that sorcerers with healing powers are used for wounds and grave diseases, not fevers—"

"Idiot woman." The Dreadlord swirled around and marched toward the door. "Summon every sorcerer in the Cursed Palace, except Andreas," he said. "Have them all converge on this room. They will not leave until they have mended what ails him."

I was near enough to hear the last words he muttered under his breath as he left the room. "I'm not ready for him to die. I'm not done with him yet."

Those words weren't a father's pained clutching to the son he loved. They belonged to a villain whose plan was not yet complete.

If I thought the bedroom was crowded before, it became even more so as the sorcerers of the Cursed Palace began to arrive. They pushed aside the physik and the attendants, plying their abilities on the Prince.

One encased him in a thin sheet of ice to cool the fever. Another stripped the Prince naked, pressed her hands to each locus on his body and made those points glow golden with energy. Her treatment had no effect, and I didn't like the way she looked at him and touched him, with a lingering sort of possessiveness. I found myself wondering if she had slept with him at any point in the past. He'd had lovers before, but until that moment I hadn't thought to be jealous of them.

Five more sorcerers did what they could, and by the power of their efforts they managed to bring down the fever. The Prince roused, blinking in disbelief at the crowd in his room, and at his own naked state. I chewed my fingernails while he scanned the circle of somber figures around his bed. When he reached my face, as I peeped between the robed bodies of the seven sorcerers, his whole expression shifted into relief and longing.

"Amarylla." He stretched out a thin hand to me, and I rushed to him, pulling the sheet over his lower half and then kissing his sharp knuckles.

"You bastard," I hissed under my breath. "I thought you were leaving me."

He laughed, thick and congested. "Not yet." He coughed, and his hand came away wet with blood.

When his eyes met mine, there was a sorrowful resignation in them. "Come here, Princess. I have something to tell you."

38

I tilted my head so my ear was near the Fiend Prince's mouth.

His voice was a ragged whisper. "Find the servant Sil. She's an airhead, but she is Onwe's cousin and knows how to reach him. I need Onwe's skill, or I may not survive this."

Under cover of kissing his cheek, I breathed, "I'll do it. I'll do anything."

When I straightened, I looked around at the seven sorcerers of the Cursed Palace—the entire retinue of natural-born magic-wielders employed by the Dreadlord. Only Andreas was missing.

What an opportunity. If only I had the poison handy, I could remove their powers, leaving them as weak and helpless as the Prince.

An idea slithered out of the darkest places of my heart, the places nearest to the poisonous truth of my name. Amarylla, named for the amaryllis flower, toxic and beautiful.

I released my most brilliant smile, the one that had dazzled the Fiend Prince himself on the night of our celebratory dinner.

"You're all so amazing," I told the sorcerers, with a breathy simper. "We have no one so wonderful in Brintzia. I'm completely in awe of your power, truly. And you've done such a wonderful job reviving and renewing His Highness! I wonder—would you all do me the inestimable honor of attending a special luncheon with me tomorrow? I'll order the very finest foods in the Cursed Palace. It will be a thank-you for your impressive work here today."

Inwardly I wanted to scream that they hadn't really fixed him, that they were useless for anything but war and damage. But I kept my saccharine smile in place, and I swept its dazzling ray over every face until their stern expressions softened a little. Grudging murmurs of acceptance—and a few enthusiastic ones—rippled along the circle of dark-clad figures.

"That's settled then!" I feigned a little wriggle of delight. "Oh, this is so exciting! Maybe you can demonstrate a little bit of magic for me, too? I would love to know who's the most powerful!"

"I'd be happy to show you some magic, Princess," said one haughty-looking woman. "If I may say so, I believe I hold the distinction of 'most powerful' in the absence of Andreas."

"You'd like to think so, Fidusa," intercepted a squat redheaded man. "But have you felled a contingent of enemy soldiers three rows deep with one conjured scythe of fire?"

"Fire isn't the greatest element, Ghorn," muttered another sorcerer. "Ice is far more effective at both immobilizing and dispatching the enemy."

"Tomorrow, then," I said loudly and cheerfully over the disgruntled mutterings.

As they filed out of the room, my smile narrowed to something that probably looked a lot less pleasant. When I turned to the Fiend Prince, he cocked an eyebrow. "You look dreadfully sadistic," he said. "What are you concocting?"

"Don't worry about it," I replied. "Rest, and get well. I'm not done with you yet." In my mouth, with the smile I gave him, the phrase was far less threatening than his father's had been. I was glad he hadn't heard those words from the Dreadlord. They might have dragged down his spirits, just when he needed every bit of his hope and willpower.

I pulled the curtains around the Prince's bed so he could rest undisturbed, and I summoned the servant Sil. She was the one who had stayed with me during my first day in the Cursed Palace, the one who wouldn't answer any of my questions about the palace or Terelaus. Today she smiled vacantly at me while I communicated the Prince's need to see Onwe.

"I will pass the word to the right people," she said cheerfully, but there was a glimmer of steel and ice in her gaze, gone so quickly I thought maybe I had imagined it. As she pranced away I wondered if perhaps her vacant good humor was a mask as solid and effective as that of the Dreadlord himself.

My invitation to the sorcerers had been impulsive, perhaps foolish, and definitely sinister. For my plan to work, I would need the toxin from that ancient monster chafing in its cell, deep in the secret parts of the Cursed Palace. Hopefully the servant I'd spoken to, the one who wanted revolution, would take advantage of the Dreadlord's absence and search his chambers. She'd served in those rooms before—she should know where to check. And now that she understood what to look for, maybe, just maybe this would work.

But no word came from her that afternoon. Onwe did not appear, and I paced the room more times than I could count, gnawing the inside of my cheek and fretting while servants whisked in and out of the Prince's bedcurtains, bringing him water and soup and handkerchiefs he could cough into. Each time they carried more bloody cloths away, my heart died a little.

From behind the black drapery of the bed, I heard the Prince say, "I will rest now, thank you. No more ministrations, I beg. Please go and tend to your other duties, or eat something, or see your families."

"Thank you, Your Highness. May the gods minister to your health," said one of the servants, and the other echoed, "May they minister."

They slipped out, with sympathetic bows to me.

The minute the door closed, the Prince called through the heavy curtain. "Amarylla."

I scrunched up my face. "Yes?"

"Would you come here, please?"

"Do you need something?"

"Only your company. I've grown fond of it. Strange, I know—you're so prickly and feral and prone to punching things. But I like it."

I sidled along the curtain, my fingertips brushing the velvety folds. "I don't do well with sick people. I don't—I can't—"

"You're strong and determined, so this kind of irreparable weakness makes you uncomfortable," he said. "You don't know what to say or do—how to fix it. So you'd rather not see it, or be near it."

My jaw dropped. How did he understand me so perfectly?

"It's not that I don't care about you," I muttered.

"I know. And I care about you as well. You're helping me be stronger where I'm weak, and that's why I'm doing this for you. Teaching you to be there for someone else, even when your strength can't help them. Even when you feel powerless." His voice was unbearably gentle, and the rattle of congestion at the end of the words broke my heart. "Open the curtains, Amarylla. Come to me."

39

Gingerly I wrapped my fingers around the curtain's edge and pulled it back, until the lamplight and firelight bathed the Prince's face and chest. In that golden glow he looked less pale, which encouraged me.

"You don't have to kiss me, or touch me," he murmured. "Just sit with me. Please. Looking at you gives me joy, and hope."

Something shattered in my head, in my heart, and I burst into tears, into harsh wracking sobs that bowed me over onto the sheets and left great wet circles where my face was buried.

The Fiend Prince stroked my hair with his long slim fingers until I was done. When I finally scraped myself together enough to look up, I saw that his cheeks were wet too. I scooted closer, to where he lay propped on the pillows, and I kissed those damp cheeks, and his forehead, and his mouth.

"Wicked prince," I said. "Cruel prince. You can't make me love you and then leave me, just when we've started scheming for your freedom, and your future. It's not right."

"I'm not dead yet, Amarylla," he said. "If willpower can keep me alive, I think yours and mine together should be strong enough. And when Onwe comes, he'll do something to help me limp along a bit further. Now sit with me, love, and tell me about your past."

We spoke of silly things at first—games of pretend we'd played as children, the few friends we'd had. Playmates were plentiful for royal children—true friends, much rarer.

Then we spoke of our mothers. Mine had died when I was a baby, and with so many kind serving women around me, I hadn't felt her loss too strongly. But Galanrae had lost his mother when he was eight.

"She went to help the victims of spotted plague," he said. "And she got too close to one of them—a small child. Her sympathy for that toddler outweighed her caution, and her love for me." He gave a sharp coughing laugh. "The last time I saw her was that morning at breakfast, before she left on her goodwill mission. Due to the threat of contagion they wouldn't let me see her again, though I screamed and threatened. I filled the hallway outside her room with thick clouds of darkness, and I lashed at the bedroom door and at the guards with whips of fire—weapons I had just learned to conjure. One of my mother's guards tried to reason with me, and I—I slashed him across the chest. He fell, with a sizzling wound right through his armor, cut open down to his spine. I nearly cleaved him in two."

I pressed my fingers over my mouth, horrified and saddened for the little prince who'd been so murderously desperate to see his mother.

"That was the first man I ever killed," said the Prince. "I stood there, shocked at what I had done—and my father swept me up in his arms and carried me out of the hall. But the Dreadlord did not rebuke me for killing a human being. He set me on my bed and smiled, and he said, 'You're not as useless as I thought. Maybe there is hope for you yet.' That was the first bit of approval and attention I'd received from him, and it came in the moment of my greatest agony and guilt."

I settled my hand over his, an echo of his pain lacing through my heart. Ever since that tender age, his father's approval and pride had always been twisted up with his own feelings of helplessness, rage, and guilt. It didn't condone what he'd done over the years, but it did help me understand him.

"Thank you for telling me," I whispered.

He nodded. "I think I'll sleep a little now. Don't leave me, Amarylla."

"Never."

He slipped into sleep almost at once, and when a knock sounded at the door I hurried to open it, and to shush whoever was there.

The brown-haired servant was back, her eyes alight.

I pulled her inside and shut the door quickly. "Tell me you have it."

In answer, she pulled a tiny bottle of swirling green liquid from the bodice of her dress.

"That's the poison? You're sure?"

"I'm not *sure*," she said. "We can't be sure without testing it. But I found it inside the bedpost in his chambers, and it matches what the Dreadlord carries on his person."

"Oh, we'll test it," I said grimly. "I have the perfect opportunity for a test tomorrow. Would you agree to be one of the servers at a luncheon I'm hosting for the sorcerers of the Cursed Palace?"

"Gladly." She gave me a sly smile. "And I can ensure that the other servers are friends of the cause."

Another rap on the door, and we both startled violently. The servant tucked the poison bottle between her breasts again, just before the door opened and a hooded figure slunk inside, escorted by the servant Sil.

"Emlin?" said Sil, peering at the brown-haired woman beside me. "What are you doing here?"

"A favor for the Princess," said Emlin, with a curt nod.

"As am I." A significant look passed between the two women—a recognition that whatever they were each up to, it was dangerous, and unsanctioned by the Dreadlord.

"Be well," said Sil, and Emlin echoed the sentiment, while Onwe darted me a smile from the shadows of his hood.

When Sil and Onwe moved on toward the Prince's bed, Emlin whispered, "I won't put the poison in the wine—too obvious, and the sorcerers are a suspicious lot. I'll have it added to the soup. How quickly does it work?"

"I have no idea."

She frowned. "I'm risking a lot, doing this. You have to promise me that if it doesn't work, and I'm punished for it, you'll find another way to take him down."

"I'm hosting the luncheon," I told her. "They'll know it was my plan. If anyone is going down for it, it'll be me. I'll take the blame."

Sil peeked around the corner of the Prince's bed, eyeing us. "A lot of whispering going on over there," she said lightly.

"We're talking of pleasure, and of bed partners," I said. "I was curious about how—how women delight other women—"

"And I told her that's a private matter," interrupted Emlin. "I should return to my duties now."

With her safely out of the room, I hurried over to the Prince's bedside. Onwe had removed his hood and was applying a glowing herb poultice to the Prince's chest and forehead. The Prince hadn't roused, and the depth of his sleep concerned me.

"Will he be all right?" I whispered. "He's been coughing up a lot of blood."

"His heart is weakening faster than I expected," said Onwe. "What happened right before this episode of fever and sickness? Did anything distress him, or cause him to overexert himself?"

"Nothing. Nothing happened—except—" My fingers fluttered to my lips. "Oh—oh, gods—he and I, we—we—"

"You consummated," Onwe finished, the corner of his mouth tipping up. "I see you took my warning to heart."

"Yes, but also—I love him." The words dropped from my lips like a death knell. They tasted like weakness. "I don't want to love him. He's going to die."

"As we all are," said Onwe. "And those closer to the grave deserve love just as much as those with years of life left ahead of them." He patted my hand. "I will do what I can for him, but you should rest, Your Highness. You look exhausted."

40

I stood at the head of the luncheon table, dressed in a gown of dark blue trimmed with silver—the brightest thing I could find among the clothes appointed for me.

The luncheon had been spread in a room with actual windows—precious few of those in the Cursed Palace—and through their frosty panes shone an anemic winter sun. Earlier, I had walked past them and glimpsed the sparkling ice-coated branches of trees, and beyond those, black stone walls slick with ice, their parapets and towers glinting sharp in the sun. A stark reminder of the obstacles between me and freedom.

More obstacles to my freedom sat around the table—seven of them, all black-robed, all keen-eyed and ready to show me their power, to cement their status in the eyes of the new Princess. Not that they cared much what I thought—they were more likely concerned with how they were ranked in the minds of their peers. I hoped that their hubris would blind them to my true purpose. Pride was the most effective distraction for the powerful.

"My lords and ladies of magic, true-born sorcerers, healers of my royal husband, His Highness the Fiend Prince," I said, lifting my goblet. "Let us drink together to the health of the heir, to the Seat of Ghast, and to the most glorious and gifted among you!"

The sorcerers exchanged glances, as if trying to sort out whom I meant by "most glorious and gifted." I saw a couple of them pass a hand over their wine before drinking it—likely a magical test to detect poison. My stomach jumped with nerves, even as my heart pulsed with gratitude to Emlin for putting the toxin in something besides their drinks.

We all sipped the wine together, and when I sat down, the servants brought out the first course, a creamy soup much like the one we'd been served at the wedding celebration. My gut contorted, but I forced myself to smile and say, "So, who would like to tell me about their powers and how you have served the Dreadlord? I have a weakness for lurid stories of valor and glory and bloodshed!"

A few of them began to speak at once, voices clamoring over each other. I raised my hand and pointed to the ice-wielding sorcerer. "If you would tell your tale first, I would be grateful. But please take a moment to eat as well—I would not wish to deprive you of these fine flavors."

"You are very kind, Your Highness," said the sorcerer. I held his gaze, smiling warmly, and his stiff frozen features cracked a smile in return. These men and women were used to the vagaries and wrath of their Dreadlord, and they seemed desperate for kind words and praise. I had to steel myself against sympathy, to remind myself that the toxin would only take their powers, not kill them. I had no idea what the toxin might to do me, a woman without magic. Probably nothing. And I had to sip the soup myself, or they might notice that I wasn't eating and become suspicious.

I took a spoonful, sipping delicately, while everyone else did the same. Some of the sorcerers even dipped in for a second spoonful. The ice sorcerer swallowed his mouthful of broth and began to speak.

But I could barely listen to him. My brain kept spinning with questions: How much toxin was in the soup? How much would it take to affect these people? When would I begin to see them having symptoms—or would the effects be visible at all? The Prince's loss of his innate magic had been noticeable at once, because his superhuman strength had disappeared immediately, and his wounds had resisted healing. But these sorcerers had no outward physical traits related to their magic. How would I know if the toxin was working?

I forced myself to refocus, to listen to the ice sorcerer's tale of freezing an entire village solid. He spoke of it as his greatest achievement. "And the Dreadlord's army simply walked through the town, smashing the frozen villagers into chunks. Easiest conquest ever." He laughed, a cold, creeping sound that sent ice into my bones.

Grimly I smiled as he took another spoonful of soup, and another. This one deserved the loss of his powers, and more. The Fiend Prince took no delight in his kills, but this man reveled in the horrific deaths of defenseless men, women, and children.

Perhaps we should have put deadly poison into the soup, instead of an untested substance that we hoped might steal the sorcerers' magic. But it wasn't in me to commit so many murders at once, no matter how much those wielders deserved death.

"A lurid tale indeed," I said. "I look forward to seeing if any of you can match it. But first, does anyone know when the Dreadlord and Andreas might return? I would like to personally inform the Dreadlord of his son's recovery."

If any of the sorcerers had bothered to check on him since the fever broke, they would know I was lying, that the Prince hadn't truly recovered. They would know that his malady went deeper than a temporary illness. Perhaps some of them had realized that while treating him, and they simply didn't care. They accepted my lies because they didn't wish to be bothered with their mortally ill Prince.

"The Dreadlord said he would return by the thirteenth hour," said one of the sorcerers. "He will probably go to the Prince's chambers at once."

My smile froze. The thirteenth hour—that was a scant few minutes away. And once the Dreadlord visited his son, he would know that Galanrae wasn't healed, that he was edging closer to the brink of death. And what would the Dreadlord do then? Rage at the sorcerers who had failed to cure his son? Would he burst into this very room, right as my plan took effect—if it ever did?

I inhaled, trying to calm myself. The scent of fresh warm bread and savory soup filled my nostrils, but it sickened rather than tantalized me. This wasn't my forte, this kind of courtly drama, these toxic machinations. I'd prefer a head-on fight with the Cursed Palace guard.

What if the Dreadlord returned to Galanrae's chambers and decided that his son was entirely useless, both as a warrior and as breeding stock? What if he decided to finish the Prince off then and there, while he lay helpless in bed? I'd left Galanrae with books and tea, and promises that I'd report on the results of the poisoning as soon as I could. He had protested, claiming he was strong enough to dress and come with me—but I'd positioned guards at his bedside, with orders not to let him rise except for trips to the bathroom.

The Fiend Prince was in no state to defend himself if Andreas and the Dreadlord decided to end his life.

A spoon thunked to the table, sucking my attention back to my guests. The sorcerer who'd dropped the spoon choked out, "I—I feel—strange."

The ice wielder's hands had gone rigid, his face frozen in shock as his body began to tremble.

I wanted to stay, to enjoy what seemed to be the first hints of my victory—but I couldn't stop worrying about my husband. "Excuse me." I rose with a swift rustle of skirts. "I must—check on the next course—I'll return shortly."

"She's poisoned us," squawked a woman. "Stop her!"

Hands thrust out toward me, but the magic that sparked from them died in midair, fizzling like flames under the rain.

Untouched, I ran from the room, while the wails of the impotent sorcerers swelled behind me.

41

I burst into the back room where the luncheon courses were lined up in silver warmers, ready to be delivered. The servants stared at me, and Emlin stepped forward. "Your Highness, what is it?"

I dragged her into a corner and whispered, "They're beginning to react. I think it's working. Do you have any more of the toxin?"

"A few drops, but—"

"Give me the bottle. I have this feeling that I need to get to the Prince, before the Dreadlord returns."

"Go." She handed over the tiny bottle. "My people and I will deal with the sorcerers."

I rushed along corridors, trying to follow my memories of the way without overthinking the left and right-hand turns.

This entire scheme was clumsy and ill-conceived. If the toxin was working—and every sign indicated that it was—the sorcerers would be reduced to common people. They wouldn't be able to defend the Dreadlord or try to take over the rule of Terelaus themselves. But that didn't solve the problem of any ichor-enhanced guards who might be in the Cursed Palace. I hadn't really accounted for them—I'd been primarily concerned with eliminating the Dreadlord and his sorcerers as a threat. I'd assumed that the other guards would swear loyalty to the Fiend Prince once the Dreadlord was killed or imprisoned. But what if they didn't?

Why had I assumed I could do this? Why had I rushed into it without taking more time, thinking through every aspect of the plot, every possible sequence of events? Why hadn't I created fail-safes and backup plans?

I cursed my own name as I raced toward the Prince's quarters, arriving breathless at the door. I pressed a hand to my waist, my ribs battling the corset for deep breaths. The guards flanking the door watched me impassively as I panted, "Has anyone—entered—"

"The Dreadlord and Andreas are within, along with the Dreadlord's personal guards," said one of the sentinels.

Without waiting for more information, I burst into the room.

The Dreadlord was in full battle armor, a mountain of black metal crowned with a helm of wicked spikes. The plates of the armor were scored by blades, stained with blood, and a massive sword was slung across his back. His belt bore a screaming skull at the center, flanked by an array of bristling knives and gleaming chains. Massive claw-toed boots dented the soft carpet by the Prince's bed.

Where the Dreadlord had crossed the floor, smears of earth and blood marred the rug.

Andreas stood behind the Dreadlord, a sneer of sick pleasure on his narrow face as he watched Galanrae's thin chest rise and fall. The Fiend Prince's eyelids were closed, and his features looked frighteningly transparent.

Quickly I scanned the bodyguards in the room—four of them, all powered up with ichor, judging by their muscles. They would be tough to take down. Normal guards I could handle—like the ones who had battled me in the training room. Guards with ichor in their bodies, and a bit of combat magic at their disposal—I wasn't so sure.

If I'd planned this better, I'd have secured some ichor for myself. I could have used it just once and powered myself up to their level.

Time to face facts—I might be smart and strong, but I wasn't good at crafting foolproof plots. No use chafing about it now, though—I'd have to make up for my mistakes with luck, skill, and on-the-spot thinking.

The Dreadlord drew off his massive right gauntlet and laid a hand on his son's forehead. "He is dying," he said. "We should have taken the girl for him months ago." His helmet swiveled, his gaze apparently centering on me, though I couldn't see his eyes through the dark eyeholes. "Do you still want to know why I chose you?"

I nodded, not trusting myself with words.

"Infertility is becoming an issue among our people," he said. "With the women, in particular.

An effect caused by—well. You don't need to know the cause."

My hands curled into fists. Was this yet another side effect of the ichor?

"I wanted a bride for my son, someone physically strong, young, fertile, attractive, and of royal birth. You were the only one in the neighboring lands who fit the criteria. And your presence here ensured your father's subservience and cooperation. A good ruler always has many reasons for his choices."

"You consider yourself a good ruler?" The words slid out before I could stop myself, and a shiver raced over my body as I remembered the whip.

"Take her into the other room, Andreas," said the Dreadlord. "See if they have coupled, and whether or not she is with child. If not, we will inject her with his seed one more time before he passes."

"And if I am pregnant?" I asked.

The Dreadlord's voice was icy, cavernous. "Then I have no further use for the boy."

Andreas gripped my shoulder and forced me along, into the bathing room. He didn't use his magic—whether he was battle-weary or he simply wanted to manhandle me, I wasn't sure. His robes were scorched and torn, and through the ripped parts I could see open cuts seeping blood. He and the Dreadlord must have come here straight from some terrible battle.

"I cannot access your sacral locus through that ridiculous dress," he said. "Take it off, or I will cut it off." Lines of green magic writhed threateningly from his fingertips.

"Undo the back for me, then." I hated to turn my back to such a monster, but I did, and felt the crackle of magic as he split the back of the gown apart, ruining it. While he did that, I quickly shifted the tiny bottle of poison from its nesting spot between my breasts, tucking it inside one of the stiff cups of my corset. It pressed painfully into my breast, but as long as Andreas didn't look too closely at my bosom, he wouldn't see the faint lump it made. He didn't seem the type to lust after women—the only looks he'd ever cast my way were those of hate and disgust.

Quickly I divested myself of the ruined dress, the hoops, and the underskirts. I stood in my corset and pantalettes, as I had on the night I first climbed into the Fiend Prince's bed with the dagger his mother had given him.

Goosebumps rose on my skin at the wash of the chilly air. A hint of herbal sweetness hung in the room, a reminder of the bath I'd shared with the Prince, and I breathed it in, drawing strength from the scent.

Andreas pulled up the edge of my corset and tugged the waistband of my pantalettes down a bit, exposing my lower abdomen. I seethed through my teeth, hating him, hating the invasion of my person, my privacy.

The sorcerer rolled up his torn sleeves, coated his right hand in green glowing magic, and pressed it to my stomach, eyes narrowed in concentration as he read the flow of energy through my body.

42

Andreas's hand stayed on my stomach for a few interminable minutes while I sucked air through my teeth and forced myself to be still, be still.

"You have been with him," Andreas said, sounding a little surprised. "I'd thought it a trick. But you are as dirty and sex-addled as the servants say—his energy is fresh, and recent. No child yet, though. Which means we'll need to try once more, before His Highness expires."

As Andreas started to turn away, I plucked the bottle from my corset, ripped out the stopper, and dashed the remaining drops over his arm. The drops vanished into his open cuts and sizzled there.

He stared at his arm for a moment, a knot of confusion between his brows. "What was that?"

I didn't know how fast the toxin would work when put in direct contact with the bloodstream. Hopefully it would be quick, or Andreas would have time to kill me before it took effect. "That was something to help you heal," I lied. "A Brintzian remedy."

"That makes no sense," he said. "You weren't allowed to bring anything with you. And I recognize that liquid." His eyes widened as the truth registered. "That idiot boy told you everything, didn't he?"

"Told me what?" I blinked innocently. But when Andreas lifted his hands, I ducked under the spiraling lines of green magic and ran from the bathing room.

When no magical ropes coiled around me and dragged me back, and when a haunted roar exploded from Andreas's throat, I knew the toxin had worked. The green magic had fizzled uselessly, just like the magic of the other seven sorcerers in the Cursed Palace.

The Dreadlord lifted his great helmeted head as I stumbled into the bedroom. "What is happening?" he bellowed.

But I barely noticed him, because the Fiend Prince's dark eyes were open, fixed on me.

I gave him a quick nod. "It's happening."

"What are you moaning about, Andreas?" roared the Dreadlord, striding toward the bathing room. He cuffed me sharply on his way past, with a muttered, "What did you do, bitch?"

I staggered, my cheek stinging where the sharp gauntlet had cut me. I felt warm blood trickling along my face.

Gritting his teeth, the Prince hauled himself upright in the bed. "Amarylla, here! You'll need this." He tugged a ring from his finger and snapped off one of the twin jewels, a stone that swirled darkly iridescent. He tossed it to me, then broke off the other stone and tucked it between his lips. "Eat it, quickly."

"What are you—" But immediately I understood, and horror clutched at my heart. "No, oh no—Galanrae, you shouldn't have taken that—you're too weak! It will kill you!"

"If it does, it's for a worthy cause." He was already changing, his form thickening, muscles swelling beneath his skin.

He had swallowed a tiny dose of ichor, the thing that was killing him. And I held a second dose in my palm.

The Dreadlord's bodyguards tightened their formation around us, although they seemed unsure what to do without their lord's orders. Before they could decide to stop me, I put the gemstone in my mouth. It began to dissolve immediately, the ichor slipping over my tongue and down my throat. My body began to hum, my cells churning and heating.

"She has broken me, ruined me!" Andreas was screaming, staggering from the bathing room. "I need the cure! I need it now! I'll kill her!"

The Fiend Prince rose from the bed, his body now a solid mass of muscle, decorated with the savage twisted scar along his side. The skin of his face had begun to peel away, flaking like burnt paper, and I remembered how he'd looked on that terrible night, without his mask. The idea of his magic-rotted face did not scare me now; I was more terrified of what would happen when the ichor wore off. In his weakened state, he wouldn't be able to survive the after-effects.

"What did you say?" He stalked toward Andreas and his father. "You need 'the cure?' But you told me there was no cure. You told me there was no chance of getting my magic back."

"There is a cure," panted Andreas, clinging to the edge of the dresser for support. "Your father wanted to keep it from you—" He broke off as the Dreadlord's gauntleted hand closed around his throat.

"So many failures, Andreas," said the Dreadlord. "And I have kept track of each one. I kept you at my side only because of your traveling magic and your research skills. And now, you think you sense the balance shifting, and you would betray my confidence?" He threw Andreas violently aside. The sorcerer's head struck the bedpost and he went limp.

My brain was a red blur of change and magic, but through the haze burned a single thought—there lay Galanrae's only chance, unconscious—maybe dead. I rounded on the Dreadlord, feeling the thrum of unfamiliar energy through my body. I felt taller, broader—my limbs pulsed with power, and sparkles of red and white magic crackled across my knuckles.

But at the center of my chest, my flesh was turning raw and rancid, rotting away. This was the locus of my energy—my indomitable heart. When I looked down, part of my left breast was gone, the rest of it was exposed muscle, and tendons stretched to my fleshless breastbone. A grotesque sight, unnerving, but I forced myself to ignore it and look up again.

"You have doomed your own son to death," I snarled at the Dreadlord. And I lashed out with all the unbearable pent-up energy inside me.

Ribbons of red-and-white fire shot from my hands, from my eyes, from my exposed thumping heart. They crashed into the Dreadlord's armor, blasting him backward. His bodyguards leaped into action, slicing at me with their own magic, throwing bolts my way—and I would have been incinerated had the Fiend Prince not leaped in front of me with a broad shield. The magic crackled helplessly against its surface.

"Where did you get that?" I shouted.

"It was under my bed. And so was this." He raised his other hand, brandishing a mighty sword nearly as long as my body—a sword with a handle of carved black bone and a glowing scarlet blade. "You take the shield. The sword is enough for me."

I gulped, barely able to look at his corrupted face, the bulging eyeballs and rotted skin and the leaking hole that used to be his nose. Worse still was his forehead, where the brain matter showed through the chewed-looking gap in his skull.

Another explosion of magical energy shook the shield. I tucked my arm through the straps and held it up, peering around it to blast my own magic toward the guards.

"You're untrained in this," called the Prince to me. "But since it's your first time with ichor, you're more powerful than they are. Use that advantage!" He ducked a magical blast and rolled across his bed, coming face to face with his father.

43

Dimly I was aware of the Prince and the Dreadlord battling each other, roaring like a pair of demons, blades ringing and screeching. But I could not watch their fight. I had enough to do, fending off the Dreadlord's four personal bodyguards all at once. Every bit of training I'd ever had, all the hours I'd spend building my strength, developing my agility and resilience—it was paying off now. Yet I wouldn't have survived a moment without that magic-resistant shield, or the power boost from the pill I'd swallowed. I could see why the Prince and the other Terelonians kept taking the ichor, even if they had misgivings about it. The sensations it awakened inside me were thrilling, addictive—I was unconquerable, all-powerful, the most magnificent warrior princess to ever live.

I smashed into one bodyguard with my shield, slammed my bare foot into another's throat. Magic blasted from my toes as I kicked, and the guard fell, shaking and choking, hands locked to his neck, blooding spewing between his fingers.

Razor blades of magic sliced across my back—not deep, but I screamed as the phantom memory of the whipping resurfaced. I whirled, more uncontrolled magic rocketing from my chest, punching against the bodyguard's breastplate. Their armor was magic-resistant too, apparently. If only such equipment had been developed when Galanrae was eight, when he killed that guard. Or maybe only the elite soldiers were allowed to wear it.

I would have to aim for the weak points of the armor, the joints and crevices. Too bad I couldn't aim my magic very well. Like me, it was impatient, ferocious.

Pain from my wounds lanced across my back repeatedly as I twisted and kicked, blasted and blocked. I used the shield as both a defense and a weapon, but I was being crowded backward, near the fireplace. I seized the poker and threw it with all my might—and while my magic might have been untrained, my muscles remembered years of spear-throwing practice. The poker sank straight into the shoulder joint of one guard's armor, and he cried out in pain, bowing over. I followed up with a kick to his head, harder than I meant to—his neck snapped with a sickening crack, and he collapsed.

Two down, and two to go. With ichor flooding my body, I could fight forever. I had unlimited magic, unlimited strength. Using it was a joy—killing was a delight. I couldn't remember why I had thought it was wrong.

I fended off another onslaught of magical bolts and risked a glance at the Fiend Prince. He was still battling his father, their two great swords clashing thunderously over and over.

The door to the suite sprang open and in rushed the two sentinels assigned to guard the Prince's chambers. They had probably been listening anxiously to the noise and only just got up the nerve to enter. "Are we needed?" shouted one of them, his voice probably shriller than he would have liked.

"Yes!" I yelled. "Help me! Defend the Prince! The Dreadlord is trying to kill him!"

One of the Dreadlord's bodyguards turned away from me and slashed a whip of magic at the two newcomers, clearly unwilling to give them a chance to join my side. And while his back was turned, I threw every bit of energy I had against him—unsportsmanlike, maybe, but with my husband's life and mine at stake, I had no time for foolish courtesy. Cords of my magic sliced the armor joints behind the bodyguard's knees, and he fell with a shriek—but not before his fiery whip had split the skull of one of the Prince's sentinels. The second sentinel cried out in fury, ripped the helmet off the Dreadlord's hobbled bodyguard, and plunged a sword through the wounded man's neck.

Three dead, one to—

Agony seared my body and I looked down to see a large steaming hole through my stomach, where the Dreadlord's fourth bodyguard had sent a bolt of magic. Bits of scarlet energy sparkled at the burnt edges of my flesh. A chunk of my gut was simply—gone.

I'd been distracted. I hadn't blocked the incoming bolt and now—now there was a fist-sized hole punched all the way through the left side of my belly.

Voiceless with shock, I blinked against the pain, against the sensation of strangeness and wrongness trickling through my body.

The Fiend Prince screamed, smashed the Dreadlord aside, and leaped over fallen bodies, his great sword raised. With one mighty blow, he cut down the bodyguard who had shot me.

My arms went loose, and the shield slid from my grip. Magic juddered from my skin in savage, unpredictable bursts, and I had barely enough voice to gasp, "Stay back," to the Prince. He was scantily clad, with no protection against my unfocused energy. A tendril of red fire shot from me, toward him, but he blocked it easily with his sword and came nearer, his hideous rotted face peering anxiously into mine.

"No, Amarylla," he said. "No, not you. We'll find a healer—I'll have someone get Onwe—"

"Behind you!" I choked, and he whirled just in time to block his father's incoming blow.

But more people were flooding into the room now—the guard Betta, and Emlin, armed with a crossbow, and Onwe with green magical darts in each hand. Sil followed, bouncing twin knives from palm to palm. And there was a golden-haired man in dark purple armor, who gave Galanrae a cocky salute and said, "Respect, cousin. A full-on rebellion—I didn't know you had it in you." And then he whipped out a massive silver sword and charged the Dreadlord.

If the Dreadlord hadn't been weary from battle, they could not have overcome him even then, despite their combined power. He was a powerful warrior in his own right, without any magic or ichor at all. But he'd been fighting for hours on some faraway field, and the combat with his son had drained him. Within minutes he was disarmed, stripped of his armor and fitted with great heavy manacles. I had a fuzzy glimpse of the Dreadlord being led away, cursing, with blood pouring down his chin—and then Onwe leaned over me, muttering and touching the wound in my stomach.

My life was seeping away, but there was a tugging from Onwe, a desperate refastening of torn things.

"Can you heal her?" The Fiend Prince's voice trembled, pleading.

"I don't think so, my friend." Onwe's tone was thick with sadness. "Too much damage. I will try, but it will take everything I have, and then some."

"Not me," I whispered, gurgling through my own blood. "Fix Andreas instead."

"For stars' sake, why, Princess?" Onwe said quietly.

"He knows—the cure—for the Prince," I wheezed. "Don't—let Andreas—die—please."

Losing consciousness wasn't something I usually did. But I sensed the shadows crawling and clustering in my brain, and I didn't have the strength to fight them, not even with the ichor buzzing along my veins.

I had taken Death by the wrists, and while trying to hold back his scythe from my love, I had impaled myself.

44

Light glimmered rosy through my eyelids. Dappled light, shifting and quivering.

Pieces of my consciousness fluttered back into place, like fallen leaves settling on the surface of a quiet lake.

A familiar voice. One I hadn't heard since it whispered, "Try to discover the source of their magic."

My father.

My eyes sprang open.

And there stood my father, brightly clad in much drapery and heavy jewelry, his beringed fingers stroking his gray-flecked beard. He was speaking to someone tall and well-muscled, someone who turned his head toward me as if my newly awakened consciousness had called to him—someone whose features were dearly familiar, yet strange.

The Fiend Prince stood at my bedside, his face flawless and his skin glowing with health. No magic-rot here, and no dreadful desiccation caused by the ichor.

He was cured.

I didn't even care how—whether they'd saved Andreas or gotten the information from the Dreadlord or found the cure some other way. I was simply glad to see him alive, and looking so wonderfully well. Hot tears leaked from the corners of my eyes, drizzling down to soak into my hair.

My voice was an unintelligible croak until the Prince hurriedly set a metal straw to my lips and let me drink some water.

"Onwe healed me?" I whispered.

"Yes," said the Prince. "Or rather, he repaired the most important parts and left the rest to heal naturally, so he'd have some power left to mend the damage to Andreas's skull. The healing he did on you was not complete, not perfect, but—"

My hand traveled beneath the sheets, under the loose nightdress I wore. I felt the rough prick of stitches, the bumpy edges of mending skin. "I'll have scars."

"I'm sorry."

"I don't mind," I said. "We'll be a matched pair."

A strained glanced passed between my father and the Fiend Prince. My father leaned over me and said, "You haven't heard the best part yet. You can come home, Amarylla. The Prince has agreed to dissolve your marriage."

Blade-sharp, startling, the pain of his statement pierced my lungs. I turned panicked eyes to Galanrae, and he nodded. "You're free," he said softly.

"But—I don't want to be free," I whispered.

My father cleared his throat loudly. "You're only saying that because you've been through such dreadful things during your stay here. It's only natural that you'd be attached to the one person who showed you any kindness. Trust me, my dear—if you return home, I promise you'll have your choice of husbands. This will never happen again."

I clenched my teeth, my eyes burning into his. "You know, I should thank you, Father. Without this experience, I would never have realized what I'm capable of, how strong I really am. But you're insane if you think I will ever trust one of your promises again. I'm staying here, in Terelaus, and when you die I will inherit the throne of Brintzia. Which means our throne and the Seat of Ghast will be united."

"There's no need for that." My father paled. "The Prince has already relinquished Terelonian rule over all the lands his father conquered, including ours. He has signed treaties of peace with everyone. So there's no need for Brintzia to be tied to Terelaus any longer."

Eyebrows raised, I turned to the Fiend Prince. "You've already done all that? How long was I unconscious?"

"About a week," he said. "It's been a busy time. I bargained with Andreas and agreed to let him take the cure if he told me where to find it. So his magic has been restored, but he works for me now—under careful supervision, of course. He's been transporting me wherever I need to go to make things right."

"What about the other sorcerers?" I asked.

"You took their magic, so I'm going to let you decide whether or not to reverse that," he said. "Personally I believe they deserve the punishment. Andreas deserves it too, but I need his transportation abilities. And he's always been more willing to obey my directives than the other sorcerers were."

On the night we were married, Andreas had listened when Galanrae told him to ease up on me. And he'd threatened me with severe consequences should I cause any harm to the Prince. Perhaps the sorcerer would be loyal to his new ruler. Though I would never stop watching Andreas, and questioning his motives. I would never trust him—just like I could never trust my father again. Not for years, anyway. Not until he proved himself worthy of my faith.

At the moment, my father's expression did not inspire confidence. He looked anxious and angry. "You're coming home with me, Amarylla. Staying here, in this cold wasteland, in this horrid dark palace—it's a terrible choice."

"Really? Because I thought selling your daughter to the Dreadlord was a terrible choice. No, actually it was a betrayal of the worst kind." I managed to pull myself up a bit against the pillows, with only minor twinges of pain across my stomach. "I love Galanrae. My place is with him, if he'll let me stay."

"Who's Galanrae?" My father looked wildly around, his expression almost comical.

"The Fiend Prince, Father."

"Oh. I've never heard anyone use his real name." My father cleared his throat, his face reddening more.

"My decision is made," I said. "And now, Fiend Prince, what is yours? Will you send me home to Brintzia, or allow me to stay here and help you rebuild your shattered kingdom?"

Galanrae stared down at me, warmth and light flowing through his gaze. A half-smile played across his mouth. "I'm not sure. Do you have the necessary qualifications for being a queen?"

"I have references." I smoothed the sheet across my legs primly and fluttered my eyelashes. "Someone once told me I was quick-thinking, funny, strong, smart, beautiful, and a good fighter. 'All admirable qualities in a queen,' he said. And I've carried off my first revolution—a bit haphazard, but overall a success, I'd say. Room for improvement, but what I lack in experience I make up for with absurd amounts of energy and confidence."

"Hmm." He tapped a finger to his lips. "I suppose you could fill the position of queen. As long as you accept the fact that I'm completely indecisive, insecure, unworthy, and embarrassingly desperate for your love."

"Not a very prepossessing list of qualifications," I murmured, reaching up to touch his cheek as he bent toward me. My heart throbbed with joy at how much healthier he looked, at the flush of his cheeks and the brightness of his eyes. Not to mention the physique under his shirt and vest. That, I looked forward to seeing very soon, with less fabric in the way.

"I have no qualifications at all," he said. "And my kingdom is in shambles. The people are confused and angry. They feel betrayed."

"Good thing both of us know first-hand how they feel," I said. "We can empathize. And I firmly believe that empathy is the most vital trait for any good ruler."

45

"So you'll help me?" the Fiend Prince whispered, his lips almost brushing mine. "You'll stay in this sordid mess of a kingdom, and help me untangle the knots my father made?"

"I'll stay." I slipped my hand behind his neck and pulled him down, humming with satisfaction as that pretty mouth of his sealed over mine. Changed though his body might be, he had the same scent—sharp and bittersweet, licorice and pepper and myrrh.

I let my tongue glide over his, feeling the familiar warmth waking up my body, pooling between my legs. He planted both hands against the mattress and kissed me deeper, his throat rumbling with eager delight.

"Wife," he whispered.

"Husband," I breathed against his mouth.

"I'm still here, you know." My father's voice was frustrated, angry, but with the faintest tinge of humor. And that shade of humor gave me hope.

We kept kissing, and finally my father muttered something about getting some dinner and left the room. The instant he left, I reached for the Prince's trousers.

"Ah, no no! Naughty Princess." He shook his head, guiding my hand away. "No physical intimacy just yet, not until you've healed. Onwe made me promise."

"Fine." I pouted. And then my pursed lips gave me an idea. "Maybe I can't have that sort of fun yet, but what about you?" And I traced my mouth with a fingertip, and looked significantly at the bulge in his pants. "I have no agenda this time. I'm not paying you for information."

The Fiend Prince's cheeks reddened. "Are you sure that's something you'd enjoy?"

"Trust me," I said. "It would be a pleasure."

He glanced at the door. "I'm very busy as the new Lord of the land, but I can spare a little time."

"Tell the servants not to disturb us," I said. "And then take off every scrap of clothing you're wearing. I want to see it all."

He poked his head out to address the guards and servants. Meanwhile I moved aside the sheet and pulled up my nightdress, revealing the fist-sized circular seam on my belly. The magic bolt had shot straight through my gut. A miracle that I'd survived, that Onwe had been able to reconstruct what I lost. I would have to ask him about the details later—I was very curious about the intricacies of his healing magic.

Galanrae was back at my bedside, half naked already. Within seconds he had everything stripped off, and I could admire his splendid body. He still had the twisted scar, wrapped around his torso, and strangely I was glad of it. That scar meant something to me—something I couldn't quite express even to myself.

"You see," I said softly, touching my own scar. "We match."

He bent down and placed soft kisses along my wound, each one a tender promise that I knew he would never break. I rolled onto my side and cupped his hip with one hand, drawing him closer to my mouth. My fingers glided along his backside, pressing him firmly forward until his erect length slid between my open lips.

We worked together, finding a comfortable position, a rhythm that suited both of us. I grew surprisingly heated just from the idea of what we were doing, and while he dipped in and out of my mouth, I secretly slipped one hand between my legs while my other hand wrapped the base of his length. His left hand pushed my nightdress up, exposing my breasts, caressing and smoothing them.

After a few minutes of panting and careful thrusts, he pulled out, gasping as he came across my chest. The shock and eroticism of the act sent me straight into a climax of my own, and I struggled to lie still and not flex my stomach too much. I couldn't hide it from him—he snatched my naughty hand from its crevice and replaced it with his own, pressing warm over my folds as I quivered with ecstasy.

"Naughty Princess," he said, but through the teasing there was a real note of anxiety in his voice. "You shouldn't have done that. Are you all right?"

"Perfectly fine," I said, panting. "More than fine. Exquisitely fine. No pain anywhere."

"Well then," he said, nudging my thighs apart. "I suppose Onwe meant that we should avoid rougher kinds of intimacy. If we keep things gentle, we can enjoy ourselves. I still have a little while before I need to be anywhere. And there is one royal qualification of mine that I have yet to show you. I was saving it, you see, as a final persuasion."

"Is that so?" I was trembling, liquid with excitement, still sensitive as he slid a finger along my folds.

"Did you know that women can sometimes have more than one climax during a lovemaking session?"

My body tingled. "I didn't know."

"Indeed. And remember the first night we met, when you held the dagger to my throat and told me never to touch you?" Another gliding, tantalizing stroke, and I struggled not to buck my hips.

"I remember," I gasped.

"Did you ever think," he said, his wicked dark eyes looking at me from between my knees, "that I would be touching you like this?" And he put that fiendishly pretty mouth in a place where no mouth had ever been before.

I had never felt more opened, exposed, and vulnerable.

I had never trusted anyone so completely.

I wanted to laugh for joy, and weep with relief, and scream with pleasure at the same time. As I panted, and curled my fingers into the sheets, and whined his name while he murmured lovely things against my most private places, I knew with a sudden rush of confidence that we could do this, he and I. His weakness to my strength, and my vulnerability to his power. We were a well-matched pair.

My father had promised that I'd marry my heart's choice. That promise was twisted, and yet in some perverted, perfect way, it held true.

My devil, my fiend, the Crown Prince of Terelaus. My husband.

My choice.

THE END

Also by REBECCA F. KENNEY

The Teeth in the Tide (Savage Seas Book 1)
The Demons in the Deep (Savage Seas Book 2)

These Wretched Wings (A Savage Seas Universe novel)

The KORRIGAN trilogy
Korrigan (Book 1), *Druid* (Book 2), and *Samhain* (Book 3)

The Monsters of Music (a gender-swapped Phantom of the Opera retelling)

Her Dreadful Will (coming April 2022)

The ASHTON SHIFTERS adult fantasy romance series

Lion Aflame (Ashton Shifters Book One)
Panther Ensnared (Ashton Shifters Book Two)

The DARK RULERS adult fantasy romance series

Bride to the Fiend Prince
Captive of the Pirate King
Prize of the Warlord

The IMMORTAL WARRIORS adult fantasy romance series

The Horseman of Sleepy Hollow

Jack Frost

The Gargoyle Prince

Wendy, Darling (Neverland Fae Book 1)
Captain Pan (Neverland Fae Book 2)

Hades: God of the Dead (coming September 2021)
Apollo: God of the Sun (coming 2022)

Printed in Great Britain
by Amazon